Forgotten

Airports will never feel the same

By Padraic Regan

For Miriam, Shauna and Kate

TABLE OF CONTENTS

Prologue

The first blow was unexpected, brutal, loud, and painful...so, so painful. To another part of the head, the second hit coincided with a massive noise as if an angry jet engine was horrified at this monstrous act. Now there was blood, blood everywhere. Thoughts were scrambled. Drifting off now. The third, fourth and fifth strikes were equally violent...but the darkness had already arrived.

Chapter 1

Eileen Gleeson was annoyed. Fifteen minutes before she finished her shift and forty-five minutes before her child-minder went on overtime with her troubled 13-year-old daughter, Kate, she had to respond to a call about a bad smell in the Baggage Reclaim Hall.

Trudging to the Baggage Hall, Eileen met several business types coming off the last flight. A mixture of male and female, they'd obviously stopped off in the bar for a quick drink and were in high spirits. Eileen envied them their freedom and the whiff of wealth that seemed to accompany them. Thinking about how different her life might have been with a college degree, she arrived in the almost deserted Baggage Hall with her mop bucket. A Sunday night in February at Dublin Airport was not a particularly hectic shift with only a handful of flights on the schedule.

She hurriedly began the well-rehearsed process of checking the area for the more obvious sources of the smell.

It could be vomit from one of the returning hen or stag party-goers; a dirty nappy thrown carelessly into one of the rubbish bins; or the carcass of a rotting rodent, partially injured by one of the many traps set during the winter months and crawling under one of the baggage belts to spend their last moments in a warmer environment.

During this specific phase of the so-far fruitless search, Eileen's eye was drawn to a lone suitcase on Belt No. 7, ambling aimlessly in a circular motion.

The display board above the belt showed a London-originating flight, but there was no sign of any passengers waiting around, and Eileen knew that such a large bag was unusual on a one-hour flight so late at night. The suitcase itself was metallic, about three feet long, two feet wide, and about one and a half feet deep, red in colour with a silver handle and, judging by the bulging nature of its deportment, over packed. The closer she got, the more confident Eileen was that her search had found the source of the smell, but that wasn't of most concern as she zeroed in on it: it was the droplets of dark red liquid that Eileen could now see clearly on the edge of the bag and dotted haphazardly along the meandering baggage belt.

Chapter 2

'Fuck off!'

Anna Jenkinson was starting her night shift at the Airport Garda Station in the same foul-mouthed, bad-tempered mood that she started – and finished – almost every shift.

'Don't worry about it AJ,' her colleague, Sergeant Tim Coady said, as he climbed into his car to head home, 'it's probably just some ignorant pet-lover, trying to smuggle their pooch in for a few days holiday'.

'Fuck off!' repeated AJ as she walked over to the Passenger Terminal, hoping that the report of what looked like drops of blood on the baggage conveyor belt would prove to be as innocent as Sergeant Coady had suggested.

The road in front of the terminal was empty except for a few taxis hoping to pick up the last of the travellers or staff finishing shifts. Temperatures were dropping all evening, and a light drizzle had started to fall, giving the well-lit front of the building a somewhat ghostly appearance in the surrounding darkness.

As AJ trudged into Arrivals, her thoughts flicked between how much she hated her job and how anyone could be so cruel or careless as to pack a pet into a suitcase.

Chapter 3

The baggage belt had been stopped, and a few staff were standing beside the suitcase when AJ arrived. One of the staff, whom AJ didn't recognise, said the bag came to her attention due to a report about a bad smell in the area.

'Did anyone touch it?' AJ asked as she looked first at the drops of dark red liquid and then at the bag itself, quickly concluding that it was a bloody big one if it was a dog.

'Not since I got here,' was the reply from a member of the Airport Police, standing protectively beside it.

The Airport Police had a lot of authority when it came to managing the flow of passengers through the airport but deferred to the Gardaí when it came to more serious, investigatory matters.

'Good,' said AJ as she finished putting on a pair of plastic gloves.

Suspicious unattended bags were not unusual at the airport. They would usually be approached expecting to find drugs or explosives uppermost in mind, but the bulky look and leakage in this instance gave it a different profile.

When the locks didn't open, AJ took out a penknife and forced the clasps. The lid sprung open, and AJ lurched backwards, reaching for her mobile phone as she stared at the bloody, unnaturally positioned, mangled corpse in front of her.

Chapter 4

'Well, well, well, look who it is! Just can't keep out of trouble, can you AJ?' smirked Detective Inspector Garoid Hennessy as he strolled towards the baggage belt.

AJ rolled her eyes; he was as arrogant as ever.

The two knew each other from the Garda Training College and subsequent assignment to the same station in Limerick. They'd lost contact after that while Hennessy climbed the promotional ladder, and AJ was in no rush to renew his acquaintance.

'Fuck off, Hennessy'.

'Tut, tut, tut, that's no way to address a senior officer AJ. Do you want to get into more trouble?'

'I hoped Head Office would take this case more seriously. They must think we found a dead poodle.'

'They wanted it solved AJ, so they sent the best. 'Now, what have you got for me?'

AJ briefed the DI as they slowly approached the suitcase, the scene having been cordoned off by the first Gardaí to respond, who were now taking statements from the staff involved.

Almost all of the airports night shift had appeared on the scene at this stage, including Customs officers and Roxy, their drug-sniffing springer spaniel. In fact, the only staff who hadn't appeared – it struck AJ – were the fire crew, air traffic controllers, cargo crew and car park operatives.

DI Hennessy listened to AJ's update while intermittently barking instructions to move staff further back, extend the taped-off area, and seal off the baggage hall.

When AJ was about to suggest that the source of the first report should also be tracked down, Hennessy cut her short.

'Thanks for your help AJ, you can go back to dealing with your pick-pockets and stolen bicycles now. I'll take it from here.'

As Hennessy leaned over to inspect the corpse, he heard the familiar voice of Calvin Walshe, one of the shift supervisors in the Garda Technical Bureau, behind him.

'Don't touch anything!'

'Thought you'd never turn up Cal,' replied Hennessy as his face creased at the sight of the suitcases gory contents. 'It's all yours; you might start by telling me the victim's gender?'

Chapter 5

AJ was cursing Hennessy as she walked back across the car park to the Airport Garda Station. Not so long ago, they were both Detective Sergeants in a busy Limerick station. The irony was that he often asked her for advice.

The memory prompted her to engage in a favoured practice, compiling fun poetry or *fhymes,* as she called them. She found it therapeutic. Her father termed it a type of Dad-joke, with too much emphasis on getting it to rhyme.

One who flatters to deceive

one wears heart upon the sleeve.

Both set out to do some good

lines got crossed, she knew they would.

'Stupid shit, he couldn't figure out a nursery rhyme,' she muttered to herself as she reflected on how his career had prospered in the past year while hers had crashed and burned. She slammed the front door of the station behind her just as the reverberations from a cargo flight's reverse thrust on landing were echoing around the otherwise quiet airport.

There were three emails in her inbox, all dealing with the forthcoming visit of British Royals the Duke and Duchess of Cambridge, Prince William and Kate Middleton. The airport would essentially be in lockdown mode for about 24 hours, with more than 100 security personnel on site before and after the visit. As with almost all-important security events at the airport, however, the local station – with just twelve staff - would play little or no part. Its meeting room and car parking spaces would be heavily used by the senior officers involved, but local officers would be pretty much side-lined.

She switched her attention to apartment-searching. Her lease was almost up, and she wasn't having much luck finding somewhere new. With one hand on her mouse, she used the other to answer a call on her desk phone. It was a supervisor in one of the aircraft maintenance hangers.

'I think our diesel thief is active,' he said.

'On my way,' she replied. For several weeks now, discrepancies were apparent in the refuelling facility for the 200-odd airfield vehicles.

These vehicles ran on a card-based system to refuel. CCTV had been installed to beef up security, but allegations of big-brother behaviour by management resulted in it being removed.

The nose cone of the Boeing 747 jumbo jet peeked out of Hanger 6 like a reluctant, caged bird as AJ approached the single pump of the refuelling facility alongside shift supervisor Dougie Farland. The parked vehicles and dark night, with rain still slashing sideways, allowed them to stay hidden while giving a decent view of the pump.

Dougie had earlier noticed a private vehicle, one with legitimate airside access but no Fleet Number, edging around the side of the hangar to park in an unofficial space.

A routine audit had brought the discrepancy to light, and AJ presumed the culprit or culprits took cards from valid vehicles, fuelled their own private cars, and returned the card, hoping nobody would be any wiser. After fifty minutes of getting wet and nobody approaching the pump, a short figure in blue overalls appeared from the hangar, got into the parked vehicle, and drove off.

Chapter 6

'Team 1 in position,' said the hushed voice over the walkie-talkie system.

'Team 2 in position,' confirmed a second voice.

'Hold your positions; wait for my command,' instructed Detective Inspector Hennessy as he surveyed the end-of-terrace house about 150 metres away through the early morning mist.

Events had moved fast since finding the body on the baggage carousel. Although no ID had been found on the victim, it was quickly confirmed that it was an Asian female in her early to mid-thirties. Death was most likely caused by multiple impacts from a blunt implement. The suitcase was still being forensically examined, but the absence of a baggage tag made it more difficult to establish its origin. Nor was it evident from CCTV footage of arriving passengers and baggage over the previous few hours who the victim was.

However, what was evident was the stooped figure of a 60-year-old Irish man exiting a bus carrying passengers from a Berlin flight. This man was known to have at least three convictions around Europe for people trafficking. As this was the only clue to emerge from the CCTV checking, Hennessy decided that it was no coincidence that a violent man was in the vicinity of a dead body that fitted the profile of his trafficked victims. When this information came to light, however, the suspect had already left the airport, so Hennessy requested a search warrant for his last known address to strike quickly before any evidence could be destroyed.

The house was in Drogheda, about 40km or 35 minutes drive from the airport, and the two upstairs lights suggested that someone was at home and awake. There were no cars parked outside, but Hennessy didn't have time to check if the suspect, Alphonsus Tobin, or Alfie to his friends, was collected by someone or had travelled by taxi.

The armed units preparing to storm the house were drawn from local stations, the Emergency Response Unit (ERU), the Garda National Drugs and Organised Crime

Bureau (GNDOCB), and the Garda National Crime and Security Intelligence Service (GNCSIS).

Hennessy insisted on national units being involved. He was confident that he was taking down a murderer and human trafficker in the same operation and wanted his success heralded throughout the force.

'GO, GO, GO' screamed Hennessy just after 3am when he was satisfied that everyone was in place. As usual in such operations, Team 1 was tasked with entering the building while Team 2 was responsible for securing its boundaries. The front and back doors were smashed in at the same time with hand-held battering rams and loud roars of 'ARMED GARDA, ON THE FLOOR!' could be heard as officers stormed in. The ground floor was quickly searched without finding any occupants, so attention moved to the first storey. Continuing the loud roars, the first two officers up the stairs ran into the bedrooms while the third opened a small storage room just off the landing. A blade flashed in front of the officer and lodged deep in the right side of her neck. Her scream of shock and pain and the sound of her hitting the laminate flooring coincided with a loud crack as her colleague used the butt of his

Heckler and Koch MP5 submachine gun to smash the head of the figure rushing out of the storeroom.

Chapter 7

AJ reflected on the speed at which bad news travels in an organisation. In contrast, the opposite was true of good news, as she heard over the radio that two people were being rushed to hospital with life-threatening injuries following a raid in Drogheda.

It brought back vivid memories of a similarly miserable night several years ago in a small housing estate on the outskirts of Roxboro in Limerick when she responded to a call from a woman reporting a missing child. The woman who made the call was Maja Nowak, a Polish immigrant living in Ireland for 8 years. Her daughter Zuzanna was 6 years old.

A windswept night, a human theft

a cry for help, a mother bereft.

No trace at first, no story to tell

no history lesson, no cruel shell.

Timing tensions, tearful flows

hopeful notices, crushing blows.

'You must know Georgina Heaslip?' AJ was startled out of her thoughts by the excited voice of Garda Morris Owens, Mossy to friends, who was sharing the night shift with her and had just returned from a foot patrol.

'Was she not in Roxboro with you before she joined ERU?' he asked,

'Yeah, I knew her but not very well. Why?' replied AJ, still bemused by Mossy's unusual level of excitement.

'She's the Guard who was stabbed up in Drogheda, lost a lot of blood and not looking good when they put her in the ambulance, I'm told.

'How do you know that?'

'Got a call from a mate in Duty Operations about hurling training on Saturday, and next thing, all hell broke loose in the office. He just rang me back a few minutes ago with an update,' spilled Mossy.

'Jesus, is he sure it's Georgina?'

'Yep, seems the blade punctured just below her helmet and just above her Kevlar vest. Serious damage is done, they're saying.'

'That's fucked up. Georgina is as careful as they come, ATLAS all the way,' exclaimed AJ, referring to the protocols established by the European Union for police tactical units after the 9/11 terrorist attacks.

'Who was the other injury?' she asked Mossy.

'Foreign national in her early 20s, can't speak much English; seems she panicked when she heard all the shouting, grabbed a knife from somewhere and hid in the closet. They think she has a fractured skull'.

'Did they find Alfie?'

'Doesn't sound like it, no one else in the house,' explained Mossy, sitting down to write his patrol report.

'So the body in the suitcase mightn't have had anything to do with Alfie?' asked AJ more in sharing her thoughts aloud than expecting a definitive answer from Mossy. He didn't respond, and after a few moments of contemplation, AJ picked up her radio.

'I'm going up to the Terminal; I'm on the radio if anyone wants me,' she said as she pondered the different case elements that didn't add up.

Chapter 8

Detective Superintendent Marie Brophy had a penchant for mixing big words with foul language. She felt it gave her the proper combination of articulation and forcefulness. Born in Virginia, County Cavan, a slight woman in her early fifties, she had jet black hair and piercing green eyes. At this early morning briefing in Brophy's office, her eyes were focussed entirely on DI Hennessy. The office had two paintings of flowers hanging on opposite walls and a framed photograph of Brophy with the Garda Commissioner centrally displayed behind the desk. Two dirty windows overlooked the staff car park. Pity she didn't merit an office with a view thought Hennessy, still upset with being summoned to the meeting when the case was in its infancy.

Also present were two Criminal Investigation detectives assigned to the case and Brophy's personal assistant, Niall McAllister, taking notes and keeping his head down.

'So, DI Hennessy, if I might commence by summarising the details of this investigation as I currently comprehend them exclaimed DS Brophy displaying clear signs of being less than pleased with matters as they stood.

'A dead woman in her early 20s was found in a suitcase on a baggage conveyor belt at Dublin Airport late last night, and within a few short hours of you being appointed to head up the inquiry, we have one ERU officer in intensive care, and one civilian receiving critical care treatment for a head wound. In addition, there are no arrests, no suspects and no leads. Forgive me for being curmudgeonly DI Hennessy, but is not the ineluctable conclusion that what we have here is a clusterfuck of biblical proportions?'

Hennessy shuffled in his chair, avoiding eye contact with anyone in the room as he tried to compose himself sufficiently to give a professional response.

'Well, Detective Superintendent Brophy,' he began, 'I felt I was acting on sound grounds to pursue the lead I had in a manner likely to bring the case to a speedy and satisfactory resolution. In fact, I still think the avenue I was following may have merit even though –'.

'Even though what?' interjected Brophy, unable to contain her anger and not sure if Hennessy was deliberately trying to mock her.

'Even though you had the barest minimum of details from forensics, or even though the incorrigible Alfie Tobin has never been known to travel on the same flight or even in the same week as any of his product, or even though the search warrant you used to storm Tobin's house gave the clear impression that you were in hot pursuit of a murder suspect when you were at best acting on a hunch. Which of those 'even thoughs' were you about to elucidate DI Hennessy?'

'None of those Detective Superintendent Brophy,' conscious among other things that the transcript of this drubbing would spread around the Force faster than most of the planes using the airport.

'I was about to say: even though it didn't pan out the way I planned'.

'Really DI Hennessy! And how exactly did you envisage it panning out? That you'd have a full fucking confession elicited from the perpetrator before breakfast and be in possession of a commendation from the Commissioner by lunch?' fumed Brophy.

'No, Detective Superintended Brophy, I didn't expect that,' replied Hennessy realising that this was a good time to shut up and take the beating.

'Good, Detective Inspector Hennessy. So here's what I suggest you do: continue your investigation by going back to the scene of the crime, find out what the CCTV, the forensics team, and the staff on duty at the time can tell you, and use the evidence derived from said sources to bring this inquiry to an expeditious denouement. Now clear the fuck out of my office so that I can brief the Commissioner and talk to Officer Heaslip's family!'

'Yes ma'am, will do,' deferred Hennessy, getting up from his chair and pretending not to notice the poorly veiled smirks of satisfaction on the faces of the two homicide detectives.

Chapter 9

A large section of the Baggage Reclaim Hall was still sealed off with crime scene tape when AJ arrived. Calvin Walshe was still beavering away, along with four of his forensic technician colleagues. A small white tent was erected over the suitcase and its grotesque contents.

The first wave of arriving flights hadn't commenced, so there were no passengers around.

'I'm under strict instructions not to converse with you, AJ,' explained Walshe when he saw AJ inspecting the area.

'From whom?' asked AJ, knowing full well the answer.

'Your former close colleague, of course. What exactly did you do to Hennessy anyway, question his parentage or something?'

'Fuck all Cal, we always got on fine in Roxboro, but he's got this superiority complex since he got his big promotion. Nothing to do with me'.

'Anyway, it's good to see you, AJ, but I can't help you with any... sorry Lubenski has arrived, gotta go', said Walshe referring to the acting Chief State Pathologist Oskar Lubenski approaching the white tent around the corpse. The man looked eager to get started on his gruesome task.

With all the attention on Lubenski, AJ ambled over to one of the technicians using an ultraviolet torch to identify trace evidence at the point where the bags emerged from the baggage hall and dispatched to the rotating conveyor belt.

'Hi, my name's Anna Jenkinson, you can call me AJ. I'm with the Garda Station here. Can I ask you if anything is showing up?' said AJ, chancing her luck.

'You can ask, AJ,' said the technician with a smile, a blond-haired tall guy who looked about sixteen, 'but I'm not telling you'.

'Why not?' cajoled AJ.

'Cos I report my findings to my boss. He decides what happens to the information then' answered the technician, continuing to perform his duties without looking up.

'Can you tell me how many crime scenes you've taped off then? That can't be a State secret?'

'That's an easy one; you're looking at it,' answered the technician.

'Seriously?' exclaimed an incredulous AJ. 'What about the baggage hall downstairs where all the sorting is carried out? And potential locations where the murder actually took place, offices, toilets, hallways? '

'Two of us spent nearly two hours doing precisely that, along with half a dozen Guards....nothing'.

'But a blood-stained suitcase can't just appear on a conveyor belt and not have left any traces anywhere else in the airport. That doesn't make sense. What about the baggage holds of aircraft that had arrived at the time; surely we've checked them?'

The technician looked up this time, but before he could say anything, his boss called him over to the other side of the conveyor belt.

As she continued her patrol around the terminal, AJ reflected on the steps involved before the State Pathologist would allow the body to be removed to the mortuary in Beaumont Hospital for the official post-mortem. There was only the dusting, swabbing and photography to complete.

She calculated that the post-mortem should be finished by the end of the day, but it could be several days before the cause of death was discovered.

Chapter 10

The baggage sorting area was a cold, cavernous building with a bare concrete floor, block walls, no windows, twelve conveyor belts and lots of circulation space for vehicles to get in and out with maximum speed and efficiency. Half the conveyor belts were for outgoing baggage and the other half for incoming with a flight information screen and electronic baggage tag reader above each one.

Attached to the side of each belt was a two-metre-wide roll of polystyrene wrap for damaged bags, along with bundles of 'Damaged in Transit' tags. CCTV cameras were scattered liberally throughout the space. Beside belt number 5 stood some electric vehicles and empty baggage dollies in a designated parking area with yellow markings. Male and female staff toilets were at one end and at the other, a few small offices and a staff breakroom.

AJ swiped her airside access card in the unit beside the door, typed in her four-digit pin, and walked into the area between belts 7 and 8. She was very familiar with the layout and operation as it was part of her regular patrols.

She noticed a huddle of four ground handling staff beside belt number 10, one of whom quickly stamped out his cigarette when he saw her, as it was a no smoking building. Staff generally tended to be suspicious of Garda patrols around the airport, and AJ knew when to try to make small talk and when to keep walking.

One of the ground handling staff peeled off from the group as AJ approached. She remembered him from an inquiry when items were reported missing from retrieved bags.

'Cold one tonight, lads,' she said as she approached.

'Busy one for you guys,' replied a tall, bald man with heavily tattooed hands.

'Yeah, looks like some unfortunate woman was murdered and stuffed in a suitcase,' she answered, taking care not to divulge any information that wasn't circulating on the gossip grapevine already.

'Heard she was cut into a dozen pieces?' ventured a young blond guy, stamping his feet to indicate he was cold and keeping his head down to avoid eye contact.

'Couldn't say,' said AJ, 'have to wait for the forensics report. I suppose you've already been questioned by some of my colleagues?'

'No,' the tattooed guy responded, 'but I saw them talking to Gibbo'.

AJ had met Tony Gibbons, one of the shift Supervisors, a few times and quickly asked if he was still around.

'Up in his office last time I saw him,' said the third man before all three zipped up their weatherproof reflective jackets and headed towards the vehicles.

The flaking grey paint on the door marked 'Shift Supervisor, TransEuro Handling Ltd had witnessed many knuckles rapping it, some with a friendly rhythm and some not so friendly. AJ's two short knocks were met with a swift 'door's open!' She pushed the door open, re-introduced herself, and asked if she could have a few words.

'Sure,' said Tony Gibbons, aka Gibbo, 'take a seat. I suppose it's about all the commotion upstairs?'

As she sat down on a green plastic seat that looked like it belonged to a fast-food restaurant, it struck AJ that the grubby door was the most attractive thing about the office. The yellowing brick walls were adorned with signs saying what not to do: 'No smoking,' 'No vaping,' 'Do not leave engines running on diesel vehicles,' 'No alcohol allowed; all branded in the top right corner with the red and grey TransEuro crest. A battered grey filing cabinet lay against the grim wall, looking lonely and unloved. The wooden desk had a phone, a notepad, a few pens standing in an old mug, and a walkie-talkie. A flight information monitor in the far corner was either switched off or had given up carrying out its task due to lack of interest.

'Thanks, yeah I understand my colleagues have already spoken to you, but I just wanted to double-check. Do you have any idea how the suitcase could have arrived on the belt without leaving any traces down here?' asked AJ as she carefully sat down, trying to avoid what looked like a fresh oil stain on the left armrest.

that operation is still in surgery, as is the girl who assaulted her. I'll update you as soon as I hear'.

'DS Brophy has ordered Forensics to prioritise their report, and our technical people are working on a photofit of the victim so we can circulate it to other airports, and Interpol and Europol.

'Our liaison colleagues began making contact with the airports served by Dublin yesterday to establish if they came across anything unusual in terms of blood stains or potential crime scenes'.

He paused to take a breath before continuing.

'No identifying marks have been found on the suitcase so far, and it looks like it's a very common make with tens of thousands sold every year. Finally, we have two lab technicians checking the hold baggage areas on planes operating into and out of here within ten hours of the body being found. This work will continue for a few days as some of the planes are overseas. I know time is vital here as traces can deteriorate or be washed off, but we don't have the authority to ground planes until they have been checked. Our job is to focus on the staff that Lockton identifies for us, some of whom we've already interviewed. We have, haven't we?' He looked around the faces, and they nodded in acknowledgement.

'For the rest, we talk to them in person either here are at their homes over the next few hours and meet back here in the afternoon to review and agree on the next steps. I will have an update from HQ by then. Everyone clear, have I left anything out?'

The two detectives from the Criminal Investigation Department nodded in agreement, and Sergeant Wang from the Divisional Drugs Unit in Swords raised his hand to get Hennessy's attention.

There was something on Wang's mind, and he wanted to get it out there.

'Just one point please, boss: why don't we include some of our people from the Airport Station? Coady, for example, knows this place inside out and knows many people here as well?'

'Over my fucking dead fucking body Wang; anything else?' spat Hennessy.

Wang's typically happy demeanour vanished at Hennessy's reaction, and he was visibly relieved when a woman's terse voice interrupted the group.

'Good morning, I'm Carmel Lockton, Head of Services here. How can I help?'

Chapter 12

After finishing her shift, AJ had one final stop to make before heading home to get some sleep.

Wearing a dark green parka over her uniform, she pulled into the car park and found a space beside the airport boundary fence. There were a half dozen other cars there, normal enough for this time of the day.

Twelve to fifteen customers were seated around the bar when she went in, almost all male, almost all airport shift staff, and almost all drinking pints. The heating was on; the intention was that the warmth and cosy feeling would make customers feel relaxed and welcome. Three TVs vied for attention, with one switched on in picture-only mode. The walls had photographs of famous visitors over the years. The floor was a dark carpet tile arrangement, allowing easy replacement when the food and drink stains became too much.

The pub was an 'Early Opener,' a pub with a special licence to open before official opening times.

Initially designed for use by dockworkers and cargo handlers finishing their night shift, the increasing use of automation and subsequent redundancies saw demand for such pubs plummet.

For many publicans, the introduction and enforcement of harsher drink driving laws proved the final nail in the coffin.

AJ wasn't there on a social call, however. She was looking for information, and she had just spotted the man who might provide it.

'Hi Larry, how are you this beautiful morning?' she inquired as she took a seat at the bar counter in front of the Guinness tap.

'Not too bad, thank you, Garda Jenkinson, and what may I ask is your poison on this beautiful morning?' Larry responded in a friendly and upbeat tone.

Larry Smalling was one of four managers in The Ark, the pub nearest the main airport entrance. He was an early riser and loved opening the pub five mornings a week, come rain or shine.

The Ark used to be called The Dark Knight after the owner's favourite Batman movie, but a massive storm stole away the D, and then The Joker was released, and the owner had a new favourite, so he got rid of the Knight.

'Just a coffee, please, Larry; busy shift last night, and I don't want to fall asleep at the wheel'.

'Coming right up, m'lady,' beamed Larry as he turned towards the coffeemaker.

AJ used the mirror behind the counter to casually check out the clientele but had made little progress in that regard when she felt a gentle fist hitting her shoulder.

'Didn't expect to see you here this morning, AJ. You could have given me a lift! Can I buy you a pint?' asked Garda Maurice Owens, standing beside AJ wearing a black blazer over his Garda tunic and holding an empty pint glass in his hand.

'Jesus Mossy, you gave me a fright!' No thanks, I'm just having a coffee and heading home. Didn't expect to see you either?' replied AJ, half turning so she could make proper eye contact.

'I'm like you, I think AJ. I only come in here in the evenings for the various wedding, promotion, and death celebrations in the force, and like this morning, when the hurling club committee meets here'. Mossy indicated three tired-looking men underneath the silent pictures of news stories on the television.

AJ politely turned to cast a glance at his sporty colleagues. There was far too much chat going on for AJ so early in the morning, so she made what she hoped was a conversation-ending response.

'Good stuff Mossy, well don't let me interrupt your deliberations, work away,' just as Larry was placing her coffee on a beer mat in front of her, along with two paper sachets of unwanted sugar and a small jug of milk.

Before Mossy could respond, the super-efficient Larry confirmed that Mossy wanted another four pints of Guinness. They would be dropped over to his table. Mossy bade AJ goodbye and went back to his mates.

As she had hoped, AJ now had an opportunity to interact with Larry as he set about the delicate and skilful task of pouring four pints of Guinness.

'So, Larry,' she said with as little purpose as she could muster, 'what's all the news?'

'Only one thing AJ, and no surprise to you: the Body in the Bag!' he answered as he held each branded glass at a 45-degree angle, slowly filling each one up to about three-quarters by pulling the tap towards him, taking great care not to let the spout of the tap touch the glass.

As many times as she had seen the process over the years, it still enthralled AJ to watch an expert at work.

'Sure, and what are they saying about it?' she asked, without taking her eyes off Larry. As a marker, he used the liquid reaching the bottom of the logo on the glass to slowly straighten the glass. When the cool black liquid reached the top of the logo, he eased off on the tap and stopped pouring.

'Just that a murdered girl arrived in off a flight last night, in a suitcase, and was only discovered when drops of blood were seen on the conveyor belt,' he answered with a grimace.

All four glasses were now sitting on a tray beside the tap to allow customers to witness the famous 'surge and settle' miracle, as the agitated nitrogen in the liquid sent 300 million tiny bubbles travelling down the glass and then back up to create the creamy head.

'Makes you wonder what kind of crazy bastard does something like that. Any of this morning's punters add any other gems of wisdom about it?' asked AJ casually, still watching the four glasses as the works of art neared completion.

'Not yet. Mind you, we've only been open twenty minutes. It's early days yet'. Larry's focus was clearly on the unfinished pints as his inbuilt timer counted two minutes until the final step was completed.

'I've no doubt we'll hear all kinds of stories as the day goes on,' he joked, holding each glass straight as he brought the head up to the rim of the glass by pushing the tap backwards.

He placed the pints on a tray and cast a critical eye over the heads to ensure they followed the 18 – 20 mm rule. He still managed to notice one of his customers approaching the bar at the other side of AJ.

'How are you this morning, Safa, the usual?' he asked warmly, without taking his eyes off the tray.

'Great, thanks, Larry, yes please, just had my easiest night shift for years,' replied a tall, gangly man with short grey hair and a moustache, still wearing dark blue overalls and black boots.

'How so?' asked Larry, passing the man as he headed towards Mossy's group.

'Brought in on overtime to service one of the baggage belts, but when I arrived in, they told me it was being used, so I spent the night reading a book, on-call. Twelve hours at double time, happy days!'

'Good for you,' said Larry, 'pint coming right up' now with his back to Safa and gently positioning each pint on Guinness beer mats in front of his four smiling customers.

'Wouldn't happen to be belt number seven by any chance?' asked AJ, conversationally.

'Ehhhh,' said Safa, unperturbed as he felt around in his pocket before pulling out a crumpled green note, 'yep, number seven'.

AJ finished her coffee, left a few euro on the counter, said her goodbyes, and drove home. She was satisfied that she didn't seem to have missed any insights circulating in the airport community, but still with many questions on her mind.

Questions and answers, puzzles and riddles, yeses and nos

leaking bags, revolving belts, blood-stained clothes.

Secrets and lies, fight or flight, fear and strife,

violent ends, murder most keen, the taking of a life.

Trust your training, look for leads, chase the clues

Validate victim, trace their trip, step into their shoes.

Chapter 13

Carmel Lockton knew airport operations inside out. She was wearing a yellow, hi-vis reflector jacket and carrying a walkie-talkie. At 51 years of age, she had recently celebrated her 30th anniversary at Dublin Airport, and she had thoroughly enjoyed each and every year.

Carmel looked more like an old-fashioned professor with brown spectacles, brunette hair in a bun, and a dowdy grey skirt. In her final year at university, studying economics and maths, an Airport recruitment poster on the Careers and Appointments Office noticeboard caught her attention: 'Try the Airport way of life' it urged. After working in a series of positions, she was now the Head of Services.

She started her tour with Hennessy and his team at the conveyor belt where the body was found. She continued to the baggage sorting area and out onto the apron where aircraft are loaded and unloaded. All the questions raised by Hennessy and his colleagues were answered clearly and comprehensively.

With almost 33 million passengers flying in and out on 230,000 flights last year, the backbone of the airport operation, she explained, was the Airport Operations System or AOS.

This software package collected and distributed information relating to passengers and cargo, from planning a flight, allocating airport facilities and services, and invoicing landings fees and other charges for that flight.

'A master flight schedule or timetable is loaded into the AOS twice a year, corresponding to the two aviation seasons: summer and winter. An operations plan for that season is then produced and discussed with airlines, air traffic control, Immigration services, freight forwarders, Customs, catering operators and ground handlers. Tweaks are made to take account of these consultations. The plan is then finalised, with adjustments only allowed when weather or other disruptions occur. The airport authority considers the system fair and transparent. However, disputes between users do arise, and accusations of bias towards certain companies have been levelled,' she explained.

Lockton pointed out the offices of the key functions on duty the night before: ground handling, maintenance, and cleaning. Hennessey's people branched off and conducted interviews. The apron area was busy with planes and their attendant vehicles coming and going, creating a constant convoy of activity. At regular intervals, the noise from aircraft taking off and landing interrupted the conversation.

Suddenly Lockton's walkie-talkie springs to life.

'Police Control: robbery reported in Cargo Terminal, landside, ongoing, white van, at least two adults. Mobile patrols respond immediately!'

Within seconds: 'Police 1 responding. In Fire Station, ETA 4 minutes.

Lockton pressed the transmit button on her unit: 'Police Control. Head of Services here. Get a camera on the forecourt and exit road quickly, please'.

The Duty Airport Police Inspector, Tony Bannon, is next: 'Police Control, API. Are the suspects armed?'

'Police Control: unclear'.

'Police Control: Police 2 responding from the holiday car park, ETA 10 minutes.'

'Police Control. Garda Station. Sergeant Coady responding will be armed, ETA 5 minutes'.

The Garda Station had an airport radio set and walkie-talkie and listened in to communications continuously, deciding themselves whether to get involved in incidents. As an unarmed force, Sergeant Coady was indicating that he would withdraw a firearm from the armoury in the Garda Station and respond to the Cargo Terminal.

Hennessy and Wang were the only two Gardaí still with Carmel Lockton. They were looking at her with bemusement.

Hennessy was first to speak: 'who the fuck is stupid enough to rob the Cargo Terminal when the airport is crawling with Guards?'

'It's mainly technical people still here, Inspector. Do you want me to respond?' asked Detective Sergeant Wang.

Lockton interjected: 'I'll get us a lift down; it's only a few minutes away'.

As the two officers and Lockton travelled to the area in an airport operations jeep, they could hear events unfold on the vehicles radio set.

Police 1 was first to arrive just as the vehicle sped away from the forecourt of the cargo terminal heading for the main airport exit towards the motorway system. An airport police officer in a four-wheel-drive jeep, Joe Tierney, knew the landscape very well and tried to cut off the escaping van by accelerating to the narrowest point of the forecourt to block the link road that joined with an office block and a fuel farm on the south side of the airport campus. Joe arrived there at virtually the same time as the white van and tried to push it against the chain-linked fence. However, the van driver anticipated the manoeuvre, braked hard, and clipped the rear driver's side of the jeep, spinning it across the van's front. Joe Tierney pressed hard on his brakes while trying to steer the jeep away from the fence but hit it side-on.

Sergeant Coady was turning on to the link road when he saw the Airport Police jeep being spun around.

Coady was driving a marked Garda car and judged his best chance of stopping the white van, now heading at speed in his direction, was to block the road with his car, stand behind it, draw his 9 mm SIG Sauer P226 weapon and point at the van using the standard two-handed shooting position.

He was still unsure if they were armed.

The van driver saw what was happening and reacted by further accelerating into the middle of the road, causing two private vehicles to take evasive action and head straight for the Garda car.

The van swung violently to the right at the last minute, hitting the rear of the car before mounting the footpath and the grass verge beyond it.

Coady had seconds to decide whether or not to open fire, but as he could not clearly see the occupants pointing weapons at him, he lowered his arms and jumped out of the way, landing on his back with a groan as he hit the concrete edge of the footpath.

When Lockton's jeep arrived at the Cargo Terminal from the airside, the emergency ramp had been activated as soon as Police 1 had gone through to prevent a car chase on the airside.

From the emergency lock position, the ramp took two coded commands and four minutes for the hydraulics to lower it into the ground again.

By that time, the white van was out of sight.

Police 2 arrived from the west side of the airport and was unable to pick up any trace of the fleeing van.

Garda vehicles from the surrounding stations had been alerted and were promptly supplied with the vehicle registration, which Joe Tierney had noted.

Hennessy and Wang first checked that no one was injured and then spoke to some of the staff involved.

The cargo operative who first noticed two adults loading the white van had challenged them because they wore hoodies with scarves over their mouths. He thought they were acting suspiciously. Although it was a cold morning, they looked like they were hiding their identity rather than seeking warmth.

They calmly closed the back doors, kept their heads down, and drove off. He couldn't see their faces clearly but said one in blue tracksuit bottoms and a black hoodie was short and stocky. The second one, wearing black jeans and a grey hoodie, was also stocky but closer to six feet six inches in height. Neither of them spoke.

While Coady was talking, Hennessy got a call and moved away, so Coady continued to discuss it with Wang, who he knew pretty well. Staff in the Cargo Terminal were checking inventories to establish what was stolen, and Police Control in the Airport Police Station was reviewing the CCTV footage.

After a few minutes, two detectives from the Robbery Unit at Ballymun drove on to the forecourt. They had already checked the registration number of the white van on the National Vehicle Registration database and established that it was fake. Nor did it look like the staff descriptions and CCTV images would help identify the perpetrators as they couldn't confirm accents or ethnicity. They spoke with Hennessy for about ten minutes when he had finished his call and agreed that Ballymun would take charge of the investigation.

Coady still held his back and looked quite uncomfortable, so Carmel Lockton gave him a lift to the Airport Medical Centre when she dropped Hennessy and Wang back to the passenger terminal.

Chapter 14

Rays of sunshine were slowly creeping out from behind grey clouds as if they were checking that the coast was clear before making a triumphant entrance. They brightened up the gloomy roadways and grass verges but weren't impacting the low temperature and chilly breeze.

AJ strolled, taking in the silence and the solitude, pausing every now and then to read an inscription. At the end of one of the many rows, she stopped, made a sign of the cross, folded her hands and whispered a prayer.

She looked out to sea, across the headstones laid flat across the cemetery, and then turned towards the older part where she could see the remnants of the original old church and a keeper's cottage.

AJ had woken up at 2.30pm, made coffee, ate a toasted ham and cheese, took a shower and put on a dark red tracksuit with white stripes on the side. It was the seventh anniversary of her mother's death, and she always tried to visit her gravestone and pay her respects. She never felt quite the same about her father's anniversary, not because she loved him less, but because he had died when she was still a teenager.

She didn't know him like she knew her mother. They were together now in their final resting place. She shed a tear as she thought about the cruelty visited on her beloved mother by bowel cancer. She still felt her parents looked out for her, albeit some days more than others.

She was in her 30s now, living alone in a rented apartment and seriously contemplating another career. She had plenty of friends to hang out with and had enjoyed her fair share of boyfriends, but she didn't feel content enough to buy a house and settle down. She knew she was attractively tall and slim, and new people always remarked on her green eyes. When socialising, she was rarely short of male attention.

I need to sort myself out, she thought as she said her goodbyes to her parents.

She had decided that having to look for a new apartment gave her the chance to have a change of scenery, so she'd made appointments to view two properties in the city centre later in the afternoon.

As she walked back to her car, listening to Cold Play's *fix you* in her headphones, her phone rang.

'Hi AJ, it's Tim, can you talk?' enquired Sergeant Tim Coady.

'Sure, Tim, go ahead'.

'Just wondering if you can come in a few hours earlier tonight, AJ, on overtime, of course?'

'Ehhh, yeah, I can change my plans; what's up?'

'Well, you're not the only one to have an action-packed shift; I heard all the gory details from last night. We had great excitement today too, and I'm feeling a bit tender after it, so I want to go home early and rest up,' said Coady.

'What happened Tim?' asked AJ, now getting very interested.

'Well, two blokes robbed a few crates from cargo in the middle of the morning. Ended up in a few cars getting damaged, me drawing my pistol, and the bastards getting away. All this with Hennessy and his crew still knocking around'.

'The fuck outta' here! No shit, so they were armed?' said AJ.

'No, that's why I didn't open fire, but I nearly did. Only decided at the last minute not to. Bastards still managed to whack the side of the patrol car and lash me into the kerb. Got some tablets in the Medical Centre here, but it's still sore,' said Coady.

AJ knew he was looking for sympathy, but she was too interested in his story to provide any.

'Jesus, that is exciting. What did they take?'

'Not a lot, according to the manifest. Machinery parts, it said, coming in from Romania last night on a cargo flight, the consignee address was fake. Ballymun lads reckon they wouldn't have risked a robbery in broad daylight unless it was drugs or guns or something. Mind you, Roxy was patrolling around cargo last night, so I'd be surprised if she missed it'.

'And what about Hennessy? Did he chase them?' asked AJ, thinking back to a few hairy pursuits she and Hennessy had been in when they worked together.

'He arrived just after they vamoosed. Seemed happy to let the Ballymun lads handle it; he has his own problems with the dead girl,' explained Coady.

'And the two cases aren't linked?' enquired AJ.

'Not as far as Hennessy is concerned, it seems'.

'Were you talking to him? Is he making any headway?'

'Talked to him briefly about the robbery, but I heard him on a call to one of the forensics people. Fingerprints aren't showing up on any database, and they're not sure DNA will be any different. Missing Persons files are not much use without a more accurate description. So they've no idea who the poor creature is or where she came from. All they know now is that she looks Asian, in her early 20s, and was cut into pieces by some form of saw or blade. He was pushing them to move faster on the DNA and cause of death, but he wasn't a happy camper,' said Coady, who knew about the frosty reception AJ had received from her former colleague when they met at the conveyor belt.

'I can imagine. Guess the botched-up house-storming didn't help matters either. He probably got an earful about it from Brophy, using words that went way over his head!'

'Anyway, I'll come in early. So you head home, Tim and take care of yourself...hero!' she grinned, now feeling much more motivated to start her next shift.

Chapter 15

When Hennessy held his review meeting with his team, it was evident that he was agitated. They had relocated to a quiet corner of the main coffee shop on the Departures floor, and the reports that were coming in from his colleagues, both those present and afar, were less than illuminating.

None of the airport staff interviews yielded any positive leads. The airport tour didn't shed any light on where the victim or suitcase originated. Contact with other airports hadn't produced any results so far. The preliminary forensic information helped little with identification. Hennessy's agitation grew as his team gave him the bad news.

The only piece of helpful information that might turn out to be useful was that an associate of Alfie Tobin had been spotted on the boardwalk in downtown Dublin. He was being followed to see if he led to Tobin.

'All in all,' sighed Hennessy, 'not a lot of progress. Any suggestions?' as he looked around his three colleagues.

It was like a school classroom: the eyes dropped to look at their notes, and papers were shuffled vigorously to give the impression of deep thought.

An exceptionally long fifteen seconds passed before Jenny Pilger broke the silence.

'CCTV', she said with some assurance.

The three men sitting around her looked bemused.

'Go on,' said Hennessy, eager to take any advice going.

'The first trawl we did of the CCTV footage last night was very hurried with only a vague description of who we were looking for. For example, the Heathrow flight that we looked at first had several people that might have been possible suspects, but when they're wearing hats and beanies and even sunglasses, it makes the task difficult. If we push the technical people for more details on height, weight, age, and a photo fit, we could do a more thorough job. Plus, our focus last night was on passengers arriving on planes, but we need to include all passengers, whether arriving by plane, bus, car or taxi. I mean, surely there are only two possibilities here: either the victim arrived at the airport in the suitcase, or she was killed and put in the suitcase at the airport?'

Jenny sat back in her seat, delighted with her contribution, and waited for a response.

'Well, that's not entirely true, Jenny,' said Detective Lucas Hannon in a belittling tone, eager to impress Hennessy and not let Pilger make him look bad.

'We did have an excellent description of the suitcase, and we couldn't find any trace of it'.

'I know, but we concentrated almost entirely on bags arriving off flights. Only a few of the cameras covered other areas,' said Pilger, not letting Hannon away with it.

'Well, Jenny.' started Hannon, but he was quickly interrupted by Hennessy.

'Okay, okay! It's not a fucking competition! Pilger's right. I'll get back on to the techies; you three go over the tapes again. Let me know as soon as anything turns up.'

Hennessy was already on his feet, dialling a number on his phone.

Chapter 16

The primary users of the boardwalk along the river Liffey in Dublin city centre rotate from season to season between tourists admiring the views and drug addicts looking for their next fix.

Ger Cosgrave was neither. He was looking for someone.

Cosgrave was a short, stocky, violent man with a tattoo of a fist smashing a door under his right ear. Cosgrave was well known to Gardaí as agnostic when it came to the type of crime, he engaged in. Drugs, prostitution, armed robberies, people trafficking, protection rackets and burglaries all featured on his illustrious criminal CV.

For anyone on the boardwalk who owed Cosgrave money or drugs, their day just took on a decidedly dark tone. In fact, such was his threatening demeanour, even those who didn't owe him anything felt uneasy.

Cosgrave didn't so much walk down the boardwalk as waddle, scanning each face for recognition, tensed to inflict significant pain on the unfortunate soul he was seeking out.

When he arrived at the end of Bachelor's Walk, he continued walking past the Ha'penny, Millennium and Grattan bridges and on to Ormond Quay, checking each individual he passed without success.

At the Four Courts, he crossed the road and headed down Chancery Place. The female cyclist following him also crossed to Chancery Place but made sure to keep her distance. Garda Helen Nolan was attached to the Bridewell Garda Station behind the Four Courts and regularly patrolled the city's boardwalks in civilian clothes, sometimes on foot but mainly on bicycle. She knew Ger Cosgrave from numerous arrests and court appearances. She also knew he was often seen in the company of Alfie Tobin, who was wanted in connection with the airport murder case.

Nolan had reported the presence of Cosgrave on the boardwalk and was told to follow him. She was familiar with this part of the city, and her cycling gear made it difficult for anyone to recognise her, particularly with the dark green helmet and visor.

When Cosgrave pressed the bell of a front door just past the pub on Chancery Place, Nolan discretely took out her radio set and reported that he was entering the offices of Stockdale, Hasson and Morrissey, the well-known firm of Solicitors. Nothing surprising there thought Nolan as Cosgrave needed solicitors as frequently as most people needed food.

Twenty minutes later, he was out again, crossed Chancery Street and headed up Greek Street. Nolan followed at a distance and stopped to untie and retie her right lace when he stopped at a block of apartments and started shouting at someone over the intercom on the wall beside the entrance.

At the same time, a dark grey Citroen saloon car pulled into the kerb twenty metres behind Nolan. The driver was in his thirties, black and sporting a crew cut hairstyle. He turned off the engine and unwrapped a stick of gum, looking out the windscreen but at nothing in particular.

Nolan walked her bicycle past the car, locked it to a signpost and sat in the passenger seat.

'Glad you got here when you did Stoksie. I felt too noticeable standing around, and I couldn't hear what he was saying anyway,' said Nolan without looking at her colleague Garda Toby Stokes.

'My pleasure Helen,' replied her gum-chewing friend. 'I headed over here when he was in with the solicitors. He has a case coming up on Friday'.

'Figured,' said Helen, what's he up for?'

'Would you believe cybercrime?' responded Stoksie with a smirk appearing on his face but still keeping his eyes on Cosgrave.

'Cybercrime? Cosgrave? But he's thick as a plank; he wouldn't know a computer from a washing machine!' Nolan looked straight ahead.

'He hit a guy over the head with a laptop last year in a pub. Said the victim was making too much noise typing on it. Poor fella had to get eight stitches in his forehead,' said a smiling Stoksie.

As Nolan was about to answer, a man in a black hoodie appeared at the entrance to the apartment block, handed Cosgrave a small package, and disappeared again.

Nolan and Stoksie spoke at the same time. 'That looked like Alfie Tobin'.

Chapter 17

When the rusty metal warehouse door finally creaked noisily into its closed position, the two occupants of the silver estate car got out and swung open the back door. Inside was a black tarpaulin and under that sat two wooden crates.

'Any trouble?' asked a man standing in front of a small office at the side of the building. He was unshaven, over six feet tall, looked like he worked out daily and spoke in an Eastern European accent.

'No, piece of cake,' answered the taller of the two men as he pulled the tarpaulin off the boxes.

They had travelled west when they left the airport and pulled in at a layby in St. Margaret's two miles away. The silver estate was already there and transferring the two crates from the white van took less than a minute. One doused the inside of the van with petrol and threw in a match while the other started the car. They waited until they were sure the van was on fire and then continued west for another fifty minutes until they arrived at a warehouse in an industrial park beside the Curragh racecourse in Kildare.

'So how come I hear on the radio about an armed robbery at Dublin Airport and that armed Gardaí tried to block the robbers' getaway?' queried the muscly man in an accusatory tone.

'That's bullshit!' the taller man shouted back in an aggressive voice.

'We weren't armed, and a patrol car tried to block the road, but it was nothing. We weren't even followed when we left the airport and haven't seen a cop car since'.

'If you've led the cops here fuckface, I'll block your fucking head with a hammer!' stormed the muscly man striding over towards the two robbers.

'Okay, okay, Flo, maybe it wasn't a piece of cake exactly, but there was no problem getting the crates, and we weren't followed here. We're not that fucking stupid!' the taller robber defended, now speaking in a more deferential tone.

'What do you want us to do with them now?'

Florin Ardelean stopped walking, stared menacingly at the two robbers standing nervously beside the stolen silver estate car, briefly considered stabbing the two fuckwits repeatedly and chopping them up into fish food, then allowed his breathing to calm and instructed them to move the crates into the brown horsebox at the other side of the warehouse.

When they finished loading the crates, the taller man plucked up the courage to ask Florin what was in them, considering he was paying them so well to have them stolen.

Florin's stare quickly let them know that such questions were unwelcome, and the pluckiness left the taller man just as fast as it arrived.

'Not to worry,' he said apologetically, 'none of our business. So, you need anything else done, always happy to do a job for you, Flo?'

Florin Ardelean took a wad of banknotes from his back pocket, threw them at the taller robber and spat out an answer as he turned back towards his office.

'Burn the car somewhere far from here, and if you ever contact or mention my name or this address again, you'll wish you had stayed in the fucking car!'

Chapter 18

Sandra Whelan was a nerd. Her family knew it, her friends knew it, her bosses knew it, her work colleagues knew it, and she knew it. Her rimless glasses were almost buried into the computer screen when AJ came into the station. Sandra loved analysing things, figuring things out, and getting answers without getting beaten up. Safe to say, Sandra eschewed the image of front-line policing being about car chases and catching bad guys. She'd joined the Gardaí for a back-office role in desk-based investigations and had proved her worth numerous times.

'Hi Sandra, how are you?'

'Good thanks, AJ,' replied Sandra, without looking up. 'Thought you were on later?'

'Yeah, Coady asked me to come in a bit early; didn't he mention it?' asked AJ.

'Not sure, maybe he did,' said Sandra, now slightly twisting her head to the right while staying focussed on the screen, as if she was following something moving sideways.

'Still a lot of activity around the passenger and cargo terminals?' enquired AJ, referring to the body in a suitcase.

'Couldn't tell you,' replied Sandra, still ensconced in her monitor.

'You didn't include the terminals in your patrol?' asked AJ, incredulous at the lack of initiative.

'I don't do patrols,' responded a resolute Sandra.

AJ shrugged and immediately headed off to the cargo terminal. Apart from some yellow crime-scene tape at one of the side entrances and a Garda technical van parked outside, there was no indication that a robbery involving police officers and vehicles had taken place a few hours earlier. The Garda patrol car that Coady used had been towed away for more detailed analysis, and the Airport Police jeep was back in operation as it had suffered only minor damage.

The front of the building was a hive of commercial activity, with delivery vans and trucks coming and going continuously. The automatic beeping sounds of large vehicles contrasted with the regular noise from arriving and departing flights on the main runway just behind the cargo terminal.

AJ crossed the crime scene tape and walked over to the entrance beside the Garda van. There was a man and a woman in white overalls working just inside the building. AJ didn't recognise the woman, but she had seen the man a few times before. Although she didn't remember his name, she knew he was a fingerprints technician from Ballymun Station. They both looked around when they saw her approach.

'Hi, I'm Anna Jenkinson from the Airport Station; how are you getting on?' she asked, relieved that they were not working for Hennessy, so should be more generous with information.

'Depends on how you look at it,' said the male technician showing some recognition of AJ behind his white mask.

'There are dozens of finger and boot prints, but none of them look recent, and we've been told the CCTV images show the culprits wearing gloves and some form of foot coverings'.

'And no sign of forced entry? Opening up crates to find the ones they wanted? Scattering contents around? Using sharp implements, etc. etc.?' queried AJ, hoping that some lead could be established.

'Doesn't look like it,' answered the man again. His colleague had turned away and resumed her work. 'We won't know for sure, of course, until we analyse the results back in the lab. We've taken some swabs off the door and off a few containers for DNA analysis, but I'm not holding my breath, to be honest. Looks like a pretty professional job, certainly not an opportunist. We're heading over to the burned-out van they found in St. Margaret's after this, but at this rate, I don't think we'll find anything significant there either'.

'Fair enough, thanks anyway,' said AJ, spotting one of the cargo staff she knew to see talking to the female technician.

He was an elderly man with grey hair and a large stomach, wearing a yellow reflective jacket and dark denim jeans.

'Sorry to interrupt,' she said to the staff member, 'just wondering if anything new turned up since the detectives were here earlier?'

'You're grand,' he answered in a friendly tone. 'I wasn't here earlier, but I just told your colleague that I can't remember such a brazen, cheeky robbery like this before, and I'm working here nearly thirty years. We've had a few break-ins and snatch-and-grabs over the years but always in the middle of the night, and certainly not when the airport was getting high profile coverage in the media over a dead body'.

'What about your own cameras in here and your stock checks; anything that could help us there?' AJ queried, happy to talk to someone who was so chatty and so experienced in the area.

'I don't think so, no,' he answered. 'Your people took the camera tapes, but the two guys were well covered up and seemed to know what they were looking for from what I heard'.

'But that sounds like they were pretty knowledgeable surely if they knew exactly what they were looking for and where it was located? I mean, look at the size of the building and the number of boxes in it?' she asked, finding it difficult to believe that it could be done without inside help but not wishing to imply that to the helpful elderly man.

'Not really,' he explained. 'It may look fairly disorganised and open, but this airport handles over 130,000 tonnes of air cargo every year, and it's a very professional, structured operation. The warehouse is organised by category and origin of goods. If you had information on where the goods were coming from, when they came in, and what the crates looked like, it wouldn't take a genius to find them. Highly valuable goods, of course, like bullion, currency, diamonds, etc., are handled differently and stored in a more secure area, but most of those goods tend to be taken straight from the aircraft under guard to the final destination. In fact, since the arrival of the overnight delivery companies and lots of computerised systems, nothing is stored for long anymore.'

'But the two stolen crates could still have contained highly valuable contents, I presume, but just weren't labelled accordingly?' probed AJ.

'True,' he confirmed. 'The Air Waybill that accompanies each air freight consignment provides a lot of detailed information, and although Customs carry out random checks to make sure the information is accurate, it's not unknown for the system to be abused. In this case, it looks like the shipper and consignee were both fake, so it's doubtful that the contents were as labelled'.

'Still', he went on before AJ had time to ask another question, 'Customs are really on the ball these days when it comes to profiling, people and goods, so I'd be surprised if it was drugs or explosives or cash. They have dog detection teams, eighteen around the country I believe, who are great at sniffing that stuff out. There's one dog on duty at the airport most days.'

'Including last night,' chipped in AJ, recalling the springer spaniel in the passenger terminal.

'Are we sure that those two crates were all they were after?' she went on. 'Might there have been more, but they were interrupted by staff challenging them?'

'No', he replied with confidence, 'the earlier shift carried out a full inventory, and everything else was accounted for'.

'And then there's your weight,' continued the cargo handler, almost talking to himself.

'Excuse me?' asked AJ, not knowing if she should be offended or not. She hoped not; she was growing fond of this chatty individual, so unusual when a Guard is asking the questions.

'Well, planes are extremely sensitive to weight,' he went on, 'much more so than ships and trains. It's all to do with weight and balance limitations of aeroplanes; it has big safety implications, so handling companies would generally notice if containers or unit load devices were much heavier or lighter than indicated. Falsifying weight wouldn't be the smartest move for criminals to make.'

'I see', said a relieved AJ, 'so we're looking at a carefully planned theft of two locatable and identifiable crates, each measuring roughly half a square metre and weighing 65 kilograms, that are unlikely to have contained drugs?'

'That's about it,' he said as a noisy convoy of containers arrived in behind him for unloading.

She was turning to leave but had one final request.

'The last question: do you mind if I have a quick look at that air waybill?'

'It's in the office; follow me.'

Walking up to the passenger terminal, AJ was still deep in thought when she stopped at the supermarket to buy a sandwich. The smiling attendant at the check-out caught her off-guard.

'Would you like to go for a drink?' he inquired respectfully.

'Oh, sorry, but I'm seeing someone,' lied AJ trying to think on her feet.

'No, I mean if you add a drink to your sandwich and crisps, you get our meal deal price; it's great value?' explained the now beaming attendant.

'Sorry, no, I'm good, thanks,' responded an embarrassed AJ, quickly tapping her bank card to pay and hurrying out of the shop with her food.

Chapter 19

The passenger terminal was even quieter on Monday night than it had been on Sunday. Still, at least the weather was slightly better, thought AJ as she strolled over to the baggage reclaim area, trying to appear casual and disinterested.

There was just one figure in white overalls working beside belt no. 7 when AJ introduced herself, explained that she had opened the suitcase and asked hopefully if anything had shown up. Thankfully for AJ, the technician seemed willing to engage in conversation.

'Nothing new,' he said in an English accent behind his white mask. 'I'm just wrapping up here; all the action has moved to the lab and the morgue. Besides, the airport wants the belt back in operation as soon as possible. Thirty-five million passengers they're expecting this year; can you believe it? In a country with a population of five million!'

Sensing she had found a second chatty individual in the space of a few minutes, AJ moved quickly to seize the opportunity.

'So, you're into aeroplanes, yeah?' she asked the man who looked to be in his late 40s, although it was hard to be accurate given the uniform.

'Aeroplanes, airports, air traffic control, you name it. I grew up just down the road from Gatwick airport and spent many hours watching landings and take-offs from the boundary road. Aerosexuals they call us, but really it's just a hobby like trainspotting or bird watching, nothing perverted about it.'

'Sure, I know,' answered AJ, anxious to make this guy feel relaxed so he would keep talking. She knew exactly where the plane spotters gathered on Collinstown Lane next to the main runway and that there was never any trouble over there except for the odd theft from a car. She also knew that its name changed to Lovers Lane after dark but thought it best not to get into that with the aviation enthusiast.

'So, what happens now exactly in terms of analysing what you've all gathered from here?' she asked, reasonably clear from her training but eager to keep the man talking.

'Well, I'm a forensic scientist, so I focus on trace evidence and work with the other specialists in the Technical Bureau: photographers, finger-printers and ballistics, to identify anything incriminating. We also collaborate with the State Pathologist's Office to build up a picture of the deceased, a PCP,' he explained.

'PCP?' asked AJ, although she had a pretty good idea what it stood for.

'Yeah, a personal characteristics profile, you know: gender, age, ethnicity, weight, height, hair colour, length and style, any moles, scars, piercings, jewellery, tattoos, etc. Mostly approximations, in this case, considering the damage done to the poor girl,' he went on. 'The early signs are that it won't be easy to answer the Queen's Questions, I'm afraid.'

'The Queen's Questions?' queried AJ, bemused.

'Yeah, that's what the old-timers used to call them when I joined the Met two decades ago. It seems it goes back to Queen Victoria, who asked about a badly cut up female torso found by construction workers in 1888 when New Scotland Yard was built. Who was she, how did she die and who killed her?'

'So, it's not just planes; you like criminal history as well?' asked an impressed AJ.

'No, no, it's just planes! The Queen's Questions is just a term that sticks is all'.

'And were they answered?'

'They were not,' he retorted in his best Sherlock Holmes impersonation, 'the 'Whitehall Mystery' remains unsolved to this very day!'

'I'm sure the monarch was disappointed?' probed AJ, not willing to relinquish the conversation yet.

'Couldn't tell ya'; she died herself a few years later, after a 63-year reign'.

'Gosh, you're a mine of information! So, tell me, what do we know about *our* female torso?' asked AJ, moving seamlessly from history to what really interested her.

'Well, strictly speaking, it's not a torso as we have the head and limbs,' said the man, now repositioning himself more comfortably beside his work kit. 'That aside, it looks at this early stage like she was hit with a blunt implement numerous times on the head, hence all the blood. The blood pigment was dark red which indicates arterial. It also looks like she was cut up with a sharp tool as the severed edges were relatively neat. Whether the blunt instrument and the sharp tool were part of the same instrument or not, we do not know. We know that her fingerprints and DNA are not showing up on any national or international database'.

'The pathologist will examine stomach contents to establish what and when she had eaten if she was a drug mule, etc. and will also look for signs of any recent sexual activity, consensual or coerced. We know that she was petite, less than five feet tall, with brown eyes, straight dark hair, and probably no older than twenty-five. We're trying to undertake a facial reconstruction, but that requires a lot of expertise and a lot of time. In the meantime, we might strike it lucky and get a Missing Person's report filed that matches our victim, who knows?'

'And the suitcase?' asked AJ, taking mental notes and keeping the information flowing.

'The outside was wiped down, which was obviously deliberate as we'd expect to find dozens of partials on a travel bag, partial fingerprints, that is. The inside, as I mentioned, had a lot of blood and body parts, blood type O positive, which a third of the planet has. The same was true for a plastic bag or sheet that she or some of her parts might have been covered with or wrapped in. There was no barcode or product number on the case, no other contents or trace of contents. The remains just barely fitted into it, so that might suggest they had to cut her up to get it closed as that was the only bag available, but there again, maybe the killer or killers planned to decapitate and amputate her and had selected a suitcase based on her size. Detective Inspector Hennessy's people are following up the bag, but it looks like that make and model are very common. And with that, my dear,' concluded the technician in his Sherlock Holmes accent but now looking at AJ with a somewhat forlorn expression, 'I'll take my leave'.

Chapter 20

A few passengers were at the taxi rank as AJ emerged into the dark night and a couple of staff waited in the smoking area under the green awnings beside the bus stops. The huge banner hanging from the multi-storey car park celebrating the 80th anniversary of the airport's opening a few weeks ago was beginning to look a little weathered. The flowerpots spread evenly along the outside of the building had been spruced up and added a bit of colour and life to an otherwise dreary scene. AJ was aware that the actual function of the flower beds was to provide some camouflage for the concrete blocks installed in 1999 after an armed gang reversed a jeep into the departures floor and robbed the bank. Such a daring raid caused consternation on the National Civil Aviation Security Committee. Additional anti-ramming and anti-terrorism measures were promptly put in place.

The cleaning department's road sweeper was slowly working its way along the arrivals road. The driver nodded to AJ as he stopped to let her cross as she made her way back to the station. She could hear a plane performing an engine test somewhere nearby. It wasn't that loud, and she figured it was at a 'ground idle setting', as her aircraft maintenance contact, Dougie Farland, had explained to her once. 'Above idle' settings were much louder and could only be performed at designated times at the northern boundary of the airport. She couldn't resist a mischievous smirk as she thought of Dougie. His phantom fuel thief only seemed to turn up when AJ was on duty; she had checked the duty logs, and no one else in the station had ever got a call. Also, Dougie seemed to talk to her about all kinds of subjects when she turned up; she had a hunch his interest could be more than professional.

But enough of that, thought AJ. She needed to concentrate on the task at hand, even if she had to conduct her investigations discretely. She thought back to her discussion with the English forensic scientist.

Based on the assumption of ages

clear as a Russian cartoon

someone surely tore out the pages

forgotten now they're playing her tune.

Wistful to look back in history

a suspect but still no accused

we now have the Collinstown mystery

the Queen she would not be amused.

'Hey, Sandra, what's been happening; any hijackings or terrorist attacks since I've been out?' joked AJ as she bounced back into the station, full of the joys of life.

'Yeah, sure,' retorted Sandra, still not looking up from her screen, 'it's been non-stop; a tsunami of crime here since you left AJ, haven't had a second!'

'Tell me this, my analytical friend'. AJ sat at her desk and entered her password to bring her computer back to life. 'How much information can we access from the main server about an active case?'

'Officially, not a whole hell of a lot; depends on the seriousness of the case: the more serious, the less access. Unofficially, it depends on how well you know the system and how techy you are,' replied Sandra. She now showed a bit of life and lifted her head to look inquisitively at AJ.

'So,' said AJ slowly, seeing that she had Sandra's attention, 'the Collinstown Mystery'.

'The what?' interjected Sandra with a crinkled facial expression.

'The girl in the bag, the murder,' explained AJ. 'What can we find about the investigation from the main server?'

'Whoa! That's both active and *very* serious, AJ,' said Sandra. I'm not sure if we should be dabbling uninvited around those files; we'll end up in a station even quieter than this'.

'Trust me, Sandra, my learned colleague: there is no station quieter than this,' said AJ. 'Stations that have been closed are busier than this!'

'Maybe,' responded a smiling Sandra, 'but it's still a considerable risk to take, and my personnel file can't fit any more negatives on it, or I'll be chucked out'.

'Fair enough Sandra, I don't want you to get into any trouble. No worries, forget I asked,' lied AJ, trying not to show her disappointment.

The two Gardaí went about their business, and there was a deafening silence in the room for the next fifteen minutes.

Eventually, Sandra broke.

'So *if* we did go meddling in that case, what information exactly would you be looking for?'

AJ looked up from the work she wasn't doing and beamed.

Chapter 21

When Helen Nolan notified her station that she was pretty sure she and her colleague Toby Stokes had spotted Alfie Tobin inside a block of apartments, they were told to monitor the building and await further instructions.

Helen asked if one of them should follow Ger Cosgrave. He had received a package from Tobin but was instructed to focus on the building and its several entrances.

In fact, the block of apartments, a former distillery with over one hundred units, had two pedestrian and one vehicle entrance, so both officers were needed to conduct the surveillance.

Nolan retrieved her bicycle and pretended to repair a non-existent puncture at one corner while Stokes repositioned his unmarked car to the parallel street, where he could see one pedestrian entrance and the vehicle entrance.

There were numerous people in and out over the next hour, residents coming home from work, residents going out to work, and fast food and grocery deliveries. As time went on and with the light fading, it became more and more challenging to remain unobtrusive and still maintain vigilance for both officers, so they were relieved when the message came in over their radio-sets that the National Surveillance Unit (NSU) were now in position and they could head back to their station. They both remarked later how they hadn't noticed anyone taking up surveillance positions.

Detective Inspector Hennessy had been informed of developments and was in direct contact with the control centre for the NSU at Garda Headquarters in the nearby Phoenix Park. The management company responsible for maintaining the grounds and common areas of the apartment development had been contacted, but the name Alfie Tobin was not registered as owner or tenant. Hennessy knew the likelihood of Tobin's name appearing in such lists was small, and he had further queried if any of Tobin's associates were recorded, but that proved fruitless also. According to the management company, nor were there any reports of anti-social behaviour taking place in any of the units. CCTV cameras were located at all entrances, but the management company explained that they were regularly vandalised. The footage was recorded over, every 24 hours, on a loop system. New European Union data protection legislation, they explained, made it much more difficult to record citizens without their explicit permission, share such footage with third parties, and transmit images captured over a data line.

Without any information on which apartment Tobin was in, assuming of course that it was Tobin in the first place, all Hennessy could do was to keep the NSU in place and direct other officers to check CCTV footage from the surrounding retail and commercial premises to definitively identify Tobin and any individuals that might be in his company.

Hennessy updated Detective Superintendent Brophy on developments and was relieved to learn that both women injured in the unsuccessful operation at Tobin's official residence in Drogheda were out of danger and receiving post-operative care. He was particularly relieved to hear that Officer Heaslip's surgery went well, and he undertook to interview her assailant as soon as doctors approved such access.

When he finished the call with Brophy, Hennessy looked at the three team members - Hannon, Pilger and Wang sitting around the desk in his office and summed up the abortive update meeting they had just finished.

'So that's where we're at, folks; essentially, it's a waiting game now: waiting to see if we can find Tobin, waiting to see if anything turns up from the airport CCTV trawl, and waiting to get the autopsy results tomorrow. We'll wrap it up for today, but if something doesn't give soon in this case, I am well and truly fucked!'

Chapter 22

Apartment 37 was on the third floor of the distillery development facing the popular Smithfield Square. It had one bedroom, one bathroom and an open plan living room and kitchen with a balcony too small to stand on.

There were seven people in the apartment.

Alphonsus Tobin was sitting on the L-shaped sofa, cursing at someone on the phone.

'I couldn't give a fiddler's fuck what he thinks. I want the merchandise I paid for! And if it's not here in one hour, I'll go over there and kick five shades of shite out of that motherfucker!' Tobin blasted into the handset.

'Okay Alfie, I'll tell him,' replied a nervy Ger Cosgrave, 'but he thinks it's worth more now what with all that shit at the airport and at your place in Drogheda over the last few days. Tobin was about to reply when he heard a scuffle at the other end of the phone and a voice spitting: 'gimme that fuckin' thing!'

Skip McEvoy took Ger Cosgrave's mobile phone and let rip.

'Dya think I can't hear ya' Tobin, you fuckin' moron? You're about as scary as a fuckin' hamster! All your shit at the airport has messed up our business, ya' halfwit! Now get this fuckin' prick off my doorstep until I get my money!'

Skip earned his nickname from his girth and his ability to dispose of food. His stock-in-trade was drugs but similar to his caller Ger Cosgrave, he would happily engage in any illegal activity that generated a profit. Several stories were in circulation over the years concerning Skip McEvoy: that he had put more people in hospital than dysentery; that he blinded a fellow inmate with a sharpened toothbrush in Mountjoy prison when teased about still living with his mother at 50; and that his neighbours in the gentrified town of Phibsborough took turns to cut his front lawn lest they incur his wrath.

Tobin heard two thuds when McEvoy had finished his rant. The first he figured was Ger Cosgrave's phone hitting Ger Cosgrave, and the second was Ger Cosgrave's phone hitting the ground.

When Tobin looked around for something to throw his own phone at, the other six people, four female and two male, in the apartment, caught his attention. He knew they could tell that he was angry. Their shuffling demeanour with heads down staring at the wooden floor they were sitting on gave that away. But he also knew that they didn't know what he had said or to whom as they couldn't speak English.

After thinking through his current situation and the options available, he swiftly concluded that neither was ideal. By the time Ger Cosgrave arrived back twenty-five minutes later, he had decided on a plan of action.

'We go with the six Ger; it'll have to do,' he explained.

'But the deal was seven Alfie, he won't be happy,' replied Cosgrave, again showing nervousness.

'I know, I know, but it's not my fault we lost one. It's that prick Floods fault! Now get them into the van and bring them over to him. I'll ring him to explain. Then get back out looking for Flood; he must be around the boardwalk; he's a fucking junkie'.

'And what about Skip?' asked Cosgrave, still trying to wipe the image of Skip's flaring nostrils from his memory.

'Fuck that fat fuck!'

The gates of the basement car park in the old distillery apartment block silently opened. A black Toyota van with 'Cleaning with Care' written on the side in white paint slowly drove out and turned left, its lights on to navigate the dark and empty streets.

Fifty metres to the right of the gates, a small navy hatchback with a roof rack and the image of a person on the phone, bearing the logo 'Tallant's Telecoms: we hear you,' pulled out onto the road and followed.

Chapter 23

'The results of photographs of the scene, and a report on the Drogheda fiasco, and some witness interviews, and a few short updates on what's going on, but I don't see any forensic or post-mortem reports,' whispered Sandra Whelan as if she had broken into a house and was fearful of waking the occupants.

'Does that mean they haven't uploaded them yet or that we can't access them?' asked AJ, leaning over Whelan's desk to peer at the computer screen and adopting the same hushed tone as her co-conspirator.

'Mmmmm, I'm not sure. I'll have to fiddle around a bit more with the list of options. I'm not clear on where different departments upload and file their reports. I thought they'd all be under the one Case Number but then again, I've never hacked an active murder file before!' answered Whelan, her voice and nervousness rising with each sentence.

'Like I said, Sandra, blame me if anybody finds out. Tell them it was all my idea – '.

'Which it was,' interjected Whelan.

'Which it was,' confirmed AJ. 'Tell them I put you up to it, put pressure on you, threatened your unborn, wouldn't leave you alone until you did it --'

'Okay, I get it, AJ! I'm not actually sure we're doing anything illegal here. We have access to a lot of information on the main server that we rarely bother with anyway. Stuff like alerts about people that may be entering or leaving the country, stolen passports that may be used at Immigration, cars used in robberies that may be dumped at the airport, that kind of thing,' said Whelan trying to reassure herself as much as AJ.

'But we get all those alerts by email or by phone if it's urgent anyway'.

'Exactly AJ,' said Whelan, feeling more confident that she wasn't going to end her law enforcement career in a prison cell. 'But those alerts or notifications get stored on the main server as well, probably as some kind of back-up policy, in case they're needed in a court case or to defend themselves in some sort of communications cock-up'.

'But it looks to me,' continued Whelan, tapping furiously on her keyboard, 'that subsequent investigations stemming from those notifications link to the original and that we have access *de facto* to said subsequent investigation files'.

AJ thought for a minute before saying anything, trying to appear tech-savvy.

'So, say we're alerted about a POI, and they're arrested at the airport and charged with a crime. The files relating to that case can be accessed from this station?'

'Exactly AJ, a Person of Interest case that involves alerting or notifying us, means we have access through the original alert or notification to that case's files. At least that's how I think it works,' explained Whelan.

'Surely it follows then,' continued AJ more confidently, 'that the files on an investigation into a dead body found in a suitcase at Dublin airport are available to us?'

'That *should* follow, but there was no alert or notification about that case, so no starting point on our system, so to speak,' said Whelan, her belief fading a little. 'The structure of main server files as I understood it reflected the organisation structure: station, district, division and region, but maybe murder cases or any serious crimes cases are treated differently. Leave it with me, and I'll see if I can figure it out'.

'Fair enough, thanks Sandra. I mean, it's not as if we we're trying to access information to sell it or subvert the course of justice or anything like that. We're trying to assist a murder investigation,' assured AJ, as much to convince herself as her colleague.

'I know AJ, but we're not officially assigned to that case, so as soon as I come up against any unauthorised access warning signs, I'm out 'a there, pronto!'

AJ went back to her desk and looked up some of the online refresher training modules uploaded and managed by the Garda Training College in Templemore. Specifically, she wanted to study the pathology and forensics areas again, which she recalled were produced by the Office of the State Pathologist and the Garda

Technical Bureau, both of which were part of the Department of Justice and Equality.

The images and slides brought back snippets of her Detective Sergeants Crime Scene Investigation training in Templemore. In particular, she recalled the lecture given by the Chief State Pathologist, a glamorous lady who had retired a year or so ago, with regular use of concepts like NASH, the options considered by pathologists when requested to investigate the manner of death: natural, accident, suicide or homicide; Occam's razor: the simplest solution among alternatives is usually the correct one; and Locard's principle: every contact leaves a trace. The benefits of tests such as toxicology, biochemistry and histology also came to mind and gruesome crime photographs used to show the different types of injury that bodies suffer, such as bruises, grazes, lacerations, stabbings, gunshots and burning. How easy it is to puncture the skin, she thought, it being only about 3 mm thick.

Her mind drifted off to that wet night in Limerick and the missing six-year-old Zuzanna Nowak and her distraught mother, Maja. Flagstaff Meadows was the estate's name. Maja explained through uncontrollable sobbing that she had left Zuzanna playing in her wooden toy house in the back garden less than an hour earlier while she prepared her dinner. This wasn't unusual as the toy house had a roof, and the rear garden had a high wall and one locked metal gate. There was also a garden light above the back door that came on automatically when darkness fell. Wearing her favourite yellow dress with red butterflies, her child had been happily playing with her colourful dolls until her mother called her for dinner. She wasn't there.

Several other Gardaí had arrived, while AJ talked to Maja Nowak to search the area and conduct house to house inquiries. One of the officers was Detective Sergeant Garoid Hennessy, and as he had attended the three-day Serious Incident Canvas Coordination training programme with AJ in Templemore, he concentrated on the house to house inquiries.

Within forty minutes of arriving, two things were clear: Zuzanna was nowhere to be seen, and Maja and her daughter kept very much to themselves. One neighbour commented that he only knew Maja to say hello to. He had never had even a weather-based chat with her. The only visitor he ever noticed was a short, dark-haired man in a denim jacket.

When AJ went back to Maja to give her an update, she gently probed to find out if anyone acting suspiciously had been noticed recently and if there was anything different about this particular evening. At first, Maja said she hadn't seen anyone or anything out of the ordinary, but after a little more cajoling from AJ, she broke down again in tears and said she had had a big argument in the last few days with her friend, Matusz. AJ didn't want to get into the nature of her relationship with this Matusz, whether he was a boyfriend, a partner, the father of Zuzanna, etc., but she did want to find him as soon as possible.

The address given by Maja was a city centre apartment block in Limerick familiar to AJ. She quickly requested the other officers present to continue with the search and canvass while she and DS Hennessy went in search of Matusz.

'I think I've found it'.

AJ was startled out of her daydream by an upbeat announcement from Sandra Whelan.

'You've found the forensics files? You're a fantastic researcher Sandra, I –'.

'No AJ,' interrupted Sandra, 'there was no sign of those files, so I started trawling through that CCTV footage that Hennessy's team were given by the airport authority. We have a direct feed into their system'.

'Oh, I see,' replied AJ, somewhat confused and now realising what time of the morning it was as she heard the familiar low drone of the tugs towing aircraft from the maintenance hangars directly behind the station to parking stands for the first wave of departures. 'So what did you find?'

'The suitcase that the murdered girl was in'.

Chapter 24

The cleaning van being driven by Ger Cosgrave moved westwards from the city centre onto the R137. There was very little traffic; a few delivery vans on early morning rounds and five or six taxis heading for the airport with passengers booked on early flights.

Taking the second exit at the roundabout, he then turned slowly onto the Tallaght Road. He was constantly looking in his rear-view mirror and at his phone in its holder beside the steering wheel. The crack on his phone screen courtesy of Skip McEvoy was noticeable but didn't prevent him from using it. Alfie Tobin should be giving him an update at this stage. He was feeling more uneasy about this plan the nearer he got to his destination.

Cosgrave pulled into a petrol station and parked beside the car wash, turning off his headlights and checking again for any suspicious vehicles behind him.

The telecoms van that had been tailing him from the city centre broke off contact at Templeogue Road and was replaced by a silver Hyundai SUV with 'STL Deliveries on both sides and the message 'Let us do the chore, straight to your door' in smaller writing underneath. The driver noted Cosgrave's vehicle pulling into the petrol station and continued along the Tallaght Road, turning left into a small housing estate two hundred metres away.

Cosgrave contemplated ringing Alfie Tobin but decided that he would have been alerted to any change in the plan by now. The smell of body odour in the car made for a very uncomfortable environment. He was anxious to deliver his cargo and have a shower as quickly as possible.

After a ten-minute wait, Cosgrave pulled back out onto the Tallaght Road and drove carefully to the next roundabout. He took the first exit onto the N81. An ambulance passed, lights on but no siren, and took the right turn for the hospital. Cosgrave took a left onto Whitestown Way along the side of the football stadium, the home of Shamrock Rovers soccer team, and again stopped, keeping his engine running and lights on, to see if anyone was taking an interest in him.

Several cars and vans passed as he waited. None of the drivers looked at him, and he was careful not to show any interest in them.

After a few minutes, he indicated to move onto the road again, drove for a few minutes before turning left and then sharp left again into a cul-de-sac. At the end of the cul-de-sac, he inched the car cautiously into an open garage adjoining a detached two-story house with a red-brick front and a small neatly trimmed lawn at the front. The house appeared to be in darkness.

He turned off the engine and lights, applied the hand brake, got out of the car and closed the garage door behind him.

At the entrance to the cul-de-sac, an STL deliveries SUV pulled in and parked. The driver took off her woolly hat and pressed the transmit button on the radio set on the dashboard.

Chapter 25

'An acute sense of observation was the phrase used by one of our instructors during the hostage simulation in Templemore, was it not AJ?'

'I didn't spot it; Sandra did,' replied AJ dismissively.

Garoid Hennessy had driven at high speed to the airport Garda station when AJ rang him at an ungodly early hour.

'There, the second one down on the far right of that baggage cart,' said Sandra, proud of her find.

Hennessy leaned over the desk and peered closely for fifteen seconds before asking: 'how do we know that's our bag? The image looks a bit grainy to me'.

'We can't be 100% sure,' said AJ, 'but we examined it for the guts of an hour before calling you. And we reckon the combination of that model bag, that colour scheme and most importantly, that bulge, make it almost a dead cert match'.

'The chances of those characteristics appearing on the same evening that a girl was found dead make it,' she went on, 'a statistically sound conclusion in our view'.

'What time does it say on the tape?' asked Hennessy, becoming more convinced the longer he looked at it.

'Seven ten pm,' replied Sandra, still beaming with delight.

'And where exactly is it located?'

'In the baggage sorting area, beside the transit bags enclosure'.

'What's the transit bags enclosure?' he went on.

'It's a section of the sorting hall that's used to temporarily store luggage that has come in on one flight and is going out on a different flight, but that second flight isn't ready for loading yet. So, in an extreme case, a passenger – and their baggage – could have a six to eight-hour transit at Dublin between flights, particularly when one leg is long-haul,' explained AJ, showing her knowledge of airport operations.

'How do you know all this?' asked Hennessy, trying not to sound impressed. In quick succession, two text message notifications distracted his attention. He read them both carefully before turning back to AJ.

'We've had a few cases of suitcases being interfered with and contents going missing since I've been here. It is hard to prove unless caught on camera because the passenger doesn't get their bag back until it's been handled by three different airports: the airport of origin, the transit airport, and the final destination. In fact,' she went on, on a roll now, 'there could be four airports involved as some passengers from remote areas may have to transit two airports'.

'Okay, okay,' said Hennessy, 'no need to show off. So assuming that is our bag, I presume we can work backwards to see how it got there and forwards to what happened next?'

'Not exactly,' said AJ. 'The cameras in that area, as in most of the airport, are rotating. Which means they operate in sweeps of the location. That allows them to cover more territory, but of course, it also means there are gaps'.

'Time gaps, you mean?' inquired Hennessy, losing a little of his enthusiasm.

'Time and physical gaps, depending on what part of the campus you're talking about. Staff changing areas, showers, even some canteens and break areas arc off-limits to allow staff privacy'.

'Canteens are private?' exclaimed Hennessy.

'Sure, agreements between management and unions over the years. There were instances where over-zealous supervisors were timing how long certain staff took for their breaks'.

'Jesus, I've heard it all now!' he sighed.

'So, what exactly can we find out from this then, assuming again that it is our suitcase?'

'We've been working on that since we called you Gar,' said AJ. 'So far nothing; we can't spot it arriving or departing from that cart. But it's early days. You probably need to get your people involved at this stage'.

'One of two questions that I had,' said Hennessy, a little surprised that AJ had reverted to the name she used to call him when they worked together.

'Go on?' AJ prompted.

'How did you get this footage?'

'The station has a live feed from the airport's CCTV network and as part of that, access to any specific or summary tapes that we need to see'.

'Which brings me to my second question: what the fuck were you two doing looking for the suitcase in the first place?'

'That's my fault, Gar,' AJ jumped in before Sandra could say anything, even though she had had no idea Sandra was trawling through the footage. 'Because I'm the one who opened the case and I'm familiar with the airport, I wanted to see if we could help your team out. As the saying goes, *many hands make light work*, and all that jazz,' she lied.

Just as Hennessy was about to utter an expletive-laden response, he was interrupted by the station door springing open.

'Morning all, how is everyone this morning?' Garda Morris Owens was reporting for duty. He knew Hennessy to see around and knew he was heading up the suitcase murder but hadn't met him formally.

'Good morning inspector, Morris Owens, based at the station here. How is your investigation coming along? If there's anything we can help you with, just ask'.

'Thanks, we're good,' Hennessy muttered, 'I've got to go,' looking sternly at AJ as he left.

The loud noise from flight operations assailed Hennessy's ears as he walked back to his car in front of the original passenger terminal, designed somewhat ironically to look like a great ocean liner. He'd never worked in such a noisy place before.

A third question had come to mind when he saw what AJ and Sandra Whelan had unearthed but he was fucked if he was going to tell them what it was. How come the team of people I have in Phoenix Park looking at those images didn't find the suitcase?

When Hennessy had left, AJ told Mossy about Sandra's great work.

'Well done, you!' he smiled, looking at Sandra. 'I saw the unmarked car in our car park, and I thought it might be another meeting about this Royal visit they're all getting uptight about. This Royalty Protection crowd are meeting with our anti-terrorist lads all the time now'.

'They're welcome to it,' yawned AJ putting on her coat, 'I'm going home to sleep for two glorious days. Not on again until Thursday night'.

Chapter 26

'What have we got?' asked Detective Inspector Hennessy, sitting into the back of a taxi parked beside a sign that read 'Oldbawn Wood: Residents only'. Beside it was a cul-de-sac road sign. He had taken the M50 ring round from the airport and arrived in Tallaght twenty-five minutes later.

'As I said in the texts, we could identify Cosgrave driving, but we weren't sure if Tobin was in it, so we followed him to here. We're still outside the apartment building,' replied Detective Garda Niamh Hourihan of the National Surveillance Unit.

'Good work, what do we know about the house,' asked Hennessy.

'We know the owners are called Costigan, that they have no criminal record, and we think they've been in the Canaries since before Christmas. They may or may not own an apartment there. They don't have any kids, and we're trying to find out if they've let the house while they're away'.

'And it was definitely Cosgrave driving?'

'100% Inspector, we have up to date photos of Cosgrave and Tobin. Plus, there's no such cleaning company, and the registration plates on the van are fake'.

Hennessy was impressed, and as he was thinking through his next move, the house's garage door slowly began to rise.

Hourihan quickly notified her colleagues of the move.

'How many people have you got here?' asked Hennessy hurriedly.

'Two others, covering the back; it leads to some waste ground behind the football stadium'.

As she spoke, the cleaning van was reversing out and turning towards the entrance to the estate. The garage door was closing behind.

'Stop or follow?' asked Hourihan, almost taking Hennessy by surprise.

'Can we identify the driver?'

'Negative, until he gets closer'.

Hennessy was racing through the different scenarios. If it's still Cosgrave driving, has he left Tobin in the house? Is Tobin in the car with him? What if it's Tobin driving, and he spots them? He'll take off for sure. Then again, Tobin might still be back in the apartment. And what the fuck was Cosgrave doing in the house, delivering something, collecting something?

'We need a call, Inspector,' pushed Hourihan.

'Stop the car!' blurted Hennessy.

Niamh Hourihan put on her Garda hat as she started the engine and swung the taxi straight into the path of the cleaning van. In a flash, she was out of the car, her weapon drawn, calling on the driver to stop.

'Armed Gardaí!' she roared, 'out of the fucking car and on the ground, now!'

Hennessy took up a similar position on the driver's side, adopting a crouched shooting position. At the same time, he pointed his Walther P99C semi-automatic pistol at the car.

But the cleaning van didn't stop; it slammed head-on into the unmarked Garda car, knocking it backwards and crushing the false taxi marking on the bonnet.

The driver immediately jumped out and raised a firearm.

Hourihan and Hennessy were both taken by surprise but were far enough away from the collision to keep their focus.

Two shots rang out in rapid succession, and a body slumped to the ground.

Chapter 27

Detective Superintendent Marie Brophy opened the meeting on Tuesday afternoon in Conference Room No. 2, Garda Headquarters, Phoenix Park, Dublin.

'You're all very welcome to this case conference regarding the medical and forensic dimensions of the airport suitcase murder investigation. Unfortunately, our somewhat recalcitrant fucking news media have deemed it necessary to excoriate the Garda Siochana for its performance in this case. Hence, I have taken the relatively unusual step of convening this gathering. May I suggest we commence by introducing ourselves?'

Seven people sat around the large rosewood table: DS Brophy and her note-taker Niall McAllister, officers Hannon, Pilger and Wang from the investigation team, acting Chief State Pathologist Dr Oskar Lubenski, and duty supervisor in the Technical Bureau Calvin Walshe.

All having introduced themselves, Brophy asked Dr Lubenski to report his findings to date.

'Well,' he started, 'my final report is still awaiting a few lab results, but I can give you our preliminary findings. Cutting to the chase, the victim died from blunt force trauma to the head; I counted five separate blows. Time of death somewhere between six and twelve hours before found, I can't be more definitive than that. No defensive injuries, so she may have been restrained or taken by surprise. The instrument used was heavy, about four kilos, and had no sharp edges; metal most likely as there were no wooden or brick splinters found in the wounds'.

'No sharp edges, and her limbs were cut off?' interrupted Brophy.

'The amputations are secondary injuries and carried out with a sharp weapon, possibly a power tool of some sort. The injuries were relatively neat, but that's down more to the weapon used than the perpetrator, in my opinion; we are not looking for a surgeon here.

'So she wasn't tortured as some media sources suggested, the bastards?' asked Brophy.

'The amputations caused severe bleeding, but I believe the victim was dead or as good as before they were carried out. Based on the blood patterns around and within the wounds, the right arm was amputated first, followed by the right leg just below hip level, and finally the left arm. The left leg was bent into an unnatural position against the buttocks, but that was almost certainly the result of fitting her into the suitcase'.

'Hopefully, she was dead before they did that to her,' said Jenny Pilger with a look of disgust on her face.

'The two attacks on her were close together, but the head injuries came first, and whether dead or not, I doubt very much that she would have felt the second attack. More details are in my report, but I'd like to turn to my internal examination results if I may,' Lubenski continued.

'All internal organs were in good condition: no signs of any illnesses, no evidence of drug use, no recent sexual activity, and has never given birth. She wasn't malnourished and had eaten within the previous twelve to fifteen hours; cheese and tomato sandwiches and milk as far as I could tell'.

'So, looked after herself; not smuggling drugs internally, and probably not a prostitute?' asked Wang.

'There is evidence of an oral contraceptive in her system, but I would say you're probably correct, yes,' answered Lubenski.

'And her personal characteristics Doctor?' queried Brophy.

'Yes, more details in my report, but essentially the picture is that of a twenty- to twenty-five-year-old, one hundred and fifty centimetres high, fifty-two kilo in weight brunette female with brown eyes and no scars, moles or tattoos'.

'Ethnicity?' asked Lucas Hannon.

'Visually, Asian, but it's difficult to tell,' replied Lubenski.

'Surely blood type and DNA can give us ethnicity?' Hannon went on, trying to show off in front of DS Brophy.

'The relationship between race and blood is an old and controversial subject, I'm afraid,' Dr Lubenski explained. 'The American Red Cross used to segregate blood from donors according to race. For example, in World War Two, African-American blood had an 'N' for Negro on the label and was only given to African-American soldiers. This continued on for years; the State of Louisiana only banned blood segregation in 1972'.

'Thank you for the eidetic history lesson, Doctor but time is of the essence here,' said Brophy brusquely.

'Yes, of course, Detective Superintendent,' said Lubenski increasing his speed of delivery, 'there are eight major blood types, and these are determined by your genes which in turn you inherit from your parents, half from your mother and a half from your father. These can indicate certain ethnicities. Still, it's a sophisticated process and not always one hundred per cent accurate due to antigen combinations etc. We have sent material to a lab in London to undertake that analysis; it's one of the results that I'm still awaiting'.

'Many thanks, Dr Lubenski, now if we could move on to your good self, Mr Walshe?' said Brophy.

'Dr Walshe, Detective Superintendent,' corrected Calvin Walshe.

'My apologies...Dr Walshe,' lied Brophy, not feeling one bit sorry.

'As with Dr Lubenski,' Walshe commenced, 'our preliminary report has been circulated, and the final report will issue when all of the laboratory results have been received and interpreted. In short, there's nothing so far on the victim or in the suitcase to identify her. Her fingerprints are not on our database or any of the international ones that we work with. Nor is there any Missing Person report that matches her, but we're still waiting to hear back from some jurisdictions. Although there were multiple sets of fingerprints on the outside of the suitcase, they were mainly smudged partials, and none appear on our database. There were no useable fingerprints on the inside of the case either, with evidence that some form of disinfectant was used to wipe the inside and outside but not very thoroughly. Therefore, they were probably in a hurry, or it was someone who wasn't particularly good at it'.

Walshe turned over a page on the report in front of him before continuing.

'We have recovered some fibres and other material from the victim's clothing, which we're still processing. The clothes themselves were a mixture of fast fashion and higher quality items; nothing that we can use to identify her with, so far at least'.

'What about jewellery,' asked Jenny Pilger, 'if she had some high-quality clothes, she might have been wearing some expensive rings or watch?'

Dr Calvin Walshe flicked through several more pages before answering.

'All of the valuables recovered are listed in the report, and there were one or two expensive items all right: a watch and a necklace, but no inscriptions and nothing particularly unique about them. We are still checking with suppliers to try to narrow down where and when they might have been sold; you never know we might get lucky'.

The other participants could see from Walshe's demeanour that he didn't look too hopeful and that luck in a large slice would be needed to help with identification.

Wang was first to break the silence.

'Can I confirm, Doctor, that we're talking about one crime scene here: the conveyor belt?'

'Correct, we couldn't find any other evidence in the airport, on the aeroplanes we could access, or from inquiries at other airports. Just the conveyor belt'.

Another silence descended on the proceedings.

'Unless, of course, you include the house in Drogheda?' he ventured.

Everyone looked up, but Brophy got in first.

'So, there was evidence in Tobin's house connected to the murder?' she blurted out.

'Sorry, let me clarify,' Walshe quickly responded, 'there was evidence in the house but not connected to the murder'.

'For fuck's sake Walshe, what the fuck do you mean?' demanded an irritated Brophy.

'I mean – as I say in my report – there were over a dozen good fingerprints obtained in the Drogheda house, and we were able to determine with certainty—'.

'Hurry the fuck up, Walshe!' shouted a splenetic Brophy, losing her patience when Calvin Walshe paused momentarily to turn another page in his report.

'....that none of them matched those of the victim'.

The assembled audience was still digesting this information and its ramifications when a well-groomed man in an expensive-looking suit entered the room.

'Good of you to join us, Detective Inspector Hennessy. I trust you have already scrutinised the preliminary reports from these two gentlemen and realised, inter alia, that your bollocks-upped raid on Mr Tobin's house was en – fucking – tirely fucking unconnected to the investigation you were supposed to be conducting?'

Hennessy was still pulling a chair out from the table when Brophy continued.

'Can I take it then that the latest fiasco you engaged in earlier in Tallaght was also a wild fucking goose chase and that you've shot a completely fucking innocent man?'

'Yes, I have read the reports, ma'am and no, I do not believe the individual in question to be innocent, but I'd prefer to brief you in private on the latest developments if I may?' Hennessy replied, trying not to show his anger towards Brophy's disrespect, particularly as he'd nearly been killed a few hours ago.

Brophy looked at him intently before responding.

'Very well, Detective,' she answered, looking at the attendees, 'we'll conclude our case conference lady and gentlemen unless anyone has anything else to add?'

'Just that we have three people in Oldbawn at the moment, and I'll make sure that the results are available as soon as possible.' said Calvin Walshe getting up from his seat, unsure how many of the people present knew about the shooting beside Tallaght Stadium.

Officers Hannon, Pilger and Wang had been notified of the shooting. All got up in unison to exit the Conference Room, along with Niall McAllister. The latter had heard the news from various reports coming into his boss's office that morning.

Dr Lubenski collected his papers and put them back in his brown leather briefcase but appeared slightly hesitant to leave. He spoke.

'It may not be significant, Superintendent, and it is in the report, but might I just point out for the record that the imprint of the injuries on the victims head along with their impact on the cervical spine and hyoid bone strongly indicate that she was struck from behind'.

No one responded, but he could see they were considering his point as he rose from his seat and walked to the door. Then, taking hold of the handle to close the door behind him, he half-turned towards Hennessy and Brophy.

'...and she was in a seated position at the time'.

Chapter 28

Hennessy was still figuring out the significance of what Lubenski had just said when Brophy turned to him with an expectant expression.

He deliberately adopted a positive orientation when he updated her.

When the cleaning van smashed into the unmarked Garda taxi, he explained, he could see that it was Ger Cosgrave driving. When Cosgrave pointed a weapon towards Garda Hourihan, Hennessy shot him twice. One bullet hit him in the shoulder and the second in the upper arm. Cosgrave's injuries were not life-threatening, and he was currently under guard at Tallaght Hospital. Garda Hourihan was also receiving treatment for shock in the same hospital; it had been her first shooting incident.

There was no one else in the vehicle, but when officers entered the house in Oldbawn Wood, he went on, six frightened non-English speaking adults were found: four female and two male. Hennessy believed these people to be the victims of human trafficking and further thought that their fingerprints would match those recovered in Alfie Tobin's house. He had spoken to Calvin Walshe earlier and expected to have his views confirmed later in the afternoon.

Brophy knew that Hennessy had shot a man twice at the incident in Tallaght, but she didn't have all the details. Now she was beginning to see the positive side of Hennessy's investigation and was impressed that he was still on duty after shooting someone. She had drawn her weapon several times over the years but had never discharged it.

'So you've broken a human trafficking ring, Detective, good for you,' she commented.

'Thank you, ma'am. I'm also pretty sure that the girl who stabbed Officer Heaslip was part of the same group but somehow got separated from them. The medics haven't let me interview her yet, but I hope to get access later today or tomorrow. I'll also question Cosgrave when they approve it, and we still have the apartment building in town under surveillance. I'm fairly sure Tobin is holed up there and that he'll make a run for it when he hears about Cosgrave'.

'You must be knackered after the day you've had,' said Brophy trying unsuccessfully to display a softer side, 'why don't you get some rest? You have plenty of detectives on your team to delegate to'.

'I'm okay, thanks, ma'am. I've fired my weapon before but it's the first time I've actually hit someone. To be honest, I'm glad he's not dead. The internal form filling is tedious enough but those people from GSOC, they're full-on'.

'Yeah, I've heard they were,' Brophy agreed. She knew that the Garda Siochana Ombudsman Commission had a reputation for making it clear that they were independent of the force. Since they were set up in 2007, their investigations into the conduct of Gardaí had resulted in numerous sanctions and prosecutions.

'Two of them spent two hours grilling me, and that's only the beginning of the investigation. My weapon has been sent to forensics, and I can't carry one until further notice'.

'Let's call it a day then, shall we?' suggested Brophy beginning to feel a little guilty for ridiculing him in front of his colleagues earlier. But not guilty enough to apologise.

'We're also following up another promising lead, ma'am,' said Hennessy, on a roll now as Brophy gathered her paperwork. 'We've spotted the red suitcase on a trolley in the baggage hall from the CCTV footage. We're trying to see who left it there'.

Chapter 29

Early on Wednesday morning, the East Pier of Dun Laoghaire harbour had its usual busy assortment of walkers, cyclists, and joggers.

One of the joggers was wearing a dark grey top, white shorts and black gloves to protect against the chilly morning. He was about six feet tall and looked like a regular on the Pier. Having already covered the full length, he moved confidently back, passing the large library and the train station, to his small, red-brick, terraced house on a side street that ran parallel to the seafront.

Forty minutes later, he appeared with hair still wet, dressed in a pair of blue denim jeans and a black leather biker jacket. He walked back along the seafront road and turned right towards the town centre, then crossed the road and entered the shopping centre.

AJ watched him discretely as he took a window seat in a coffee shop on the ground floor. After her conversation with Doug Farland the previous day, it struck AJ that maybe his eagerness to talk to her had a more devious objective than simply working up the courage to ask her out.

Maybe he was chatting her up using a fuel thief to distract her from some other activities that were taking place at that time? Criminal activities? Or perhaps the calls were designed to figure out what she might know about various criminal acts at the airport?

Could she be that gullible she asked herself to mistake a seeming fondness for her for what were actually ulterior motives? The location of the suitcase where Sandra spotted it on CCTV and its later disappearance from the footage and then re-appearance on baggage belt number seven made it seem to AJ that someone who worked in the airport, or was very familiar with airport operations, was involved. Or maybe this girl in the bag business and the haunting scene of horribleness that greeted AJ when she opened the suitcase had made her see all of humanity's behaviour with a jaundiced eye. The decision to monitor Doug Farland's movements on this sunny, chilly morning no doubt stemmed from this view.

It was her day off, she had no plans, and she knew his home address from one of their many conversations at the airport.

He loves me; he loves me not

he's suspicious; he knows the plot

Cupid kept her powder dry

life goes on no time to cry

Scenes are not what they might seem

lonely people may act too keen

don't get soft, don't be smug

one eye open one on Doug

As Doug Farland's coffee was served after about ten minutes, he stood up to welcome two adults about his own age, a man and a woman. AJ could see the seat from a public bench across the road and, with her sunglasses and a fluffy hat, was quite confident that Doug wouldn't recognise her, even if he did look over through the passing traffic.

Doug seemed on good terms with his two dining companions. He shook hands with the man and embraced the woman as he beckoned them to take a seat. AJ didn't recognise either of the individuals and thought about trying to take photos of them with her mobile phone but decided against it because they were too far away and there was a constant flow of cars and buses on the road. She knew Doug had no criminal record and wondered if her memory would serve her to identify his colleagues, using the various image databases she had access to. The man was dressed casually and was about the same height as Doug; the woman was of colour and about a foot shorter.

When the food arrived, it looked very much like a social gathering as all three were smiling and laughing. That could be a ruse, of course, surmised a cynical AJ as she reshuffled her newspaper, tired of holding it without reading at this stage. Could they be old friends, she wondered, or might they be arch criminals along Bonnie and Clyde lines, well accustomed to acting normal in such settings?

Another hour passed, and AJ was relieved to see the waitress arrive with the bill and a card reading machine. When all three re-emerged from the coffee shop onto the street, she kept her head down and hoped they stayed on that side of the road. Instead, Doug and his friends walked back towards the harbour, crossed two pedestrian crossings and stood outside the train station for a few minutes chatting. Then Doug shook hands with the man, the woman hugged the man she arrived with, and Doug and the woman – who AJ could now see was about five feet tall, slim and in her early to mid-thirties – walked back to his house holding hands.

AJ just arrived at the corner of the road in time to see the woman take out what looked like her own set of keys to open the front door; time to rethink this, she decided.

Chapter 30

Her eyes looked vacant. That was the first thought that struck Hennessy when he entered the private room in the hospital to interview the girl arrested at Tobin's house in Balbriggan.

Then again, there wasn't much else to see of her, given the heavy white bandaging on her head that ran around her forehead and under her jaw. She lay in a prone position with her head slightly raised on a large pillow. A drip from her right arm was standing at the side of the bed, and a small locker with some water on it was positioned on the window side. Not that the girl seemed aware of anything in the room, thought Hennessy as she held her vacant stare on him.

It had taken some persuasion, and a little pressure, to get approval from her medical team to conduct the interview but Hennessy had stressed the importance of the murder inquiry. The permission granted was for a maximum of thirty minutes and must cease immediately if their patient became anxious in any way.

The girl didn't acknowledge the presence of Hennessy and the translator that he had brought with him and showed no outward sign that she was alarmed at their arrival.

Hennessy introduced her two visitors and pulled up chairs on either side of the bed. He further explained that the translator's mobile phone was to communicate with his colleagues to establish what language or languages the girl spoke. As he explained the purpose of the interview, it seemed to Hennessy that either English was not one of her spoken languages, or she was too traumatised to take in anything that had happened.

She had been formally arrested for assaulting a member of An Garda Siochana. The uniformed Garda positioned outside her room was there to prevent her from leaving and protect her from any further harm. The charge of assault was being reviewed to decide if attempted murder might be more appropriate. There was also the matter of various Immigration violations.

At Hennessy's nod, the translator began to converse with the girl in several Asian languages. Still, she didn't respond to any of them. He tried the Mandarin and Cantonese dialects of Chinese and Vietnamese before ringing a colleague who spoke Japanese, Khmer and two of the four main Thai dialects. With still no indication that she understood any of them, he asked Hennessy if he wanted a Malaysian colleague who spoke Malay and Tamil to try.

The detective had been watching her intently as the translator attempted to communicate and couldn't help feeling sorry for her. He wondered what kind of abuse had befallen her before she was arrested that night and how she had ended up in such a sorrowful and pitiful situation. She looked so gaunt and fragile, about as far from someone who wanted to seriously injure a police officer as he could imagine.

He beckoned to the translator to stand down and began to talk to the girl in a slow, sympathetic tone. He explained that he wasn't trying to cause her further harm but rather apprehend those who had brought her to that house in Balbriggan. He assured her that she was safe from those people now and that there was a police officer outside her room to make sure no one caused her further harm. Slowly he described the murder of a young girl similar to her that he was investigating. He wanted to find out anything he could about the people who had brought her to this country as they might be connected to the airport murder. He didn't think that she had intentionally attacked a police officer but that she did cause that officer a severe injury and would have to answer for it. Any information that she could give him might prove extremely useful to help prevent other young girls from suffering a fate similar to hers.

This one-sided conversation took some time, and Hennessy was conscious of his thirty-minute slot ticking away. He leaned back in his chair and let the girl continue to stare at nothing for a few minutes. Then, with the translator indicating that they were getting nowhere, Hennessy decided to have one final attempt.

He stood a few feet from the end of the bed. He told the girl that he had shot and arrested a man who could have been involved in her mistreatment and several people that she might know or have met had been rescued from a house on the west side of Dublin city. These people were being cared for by authorities, he explained, and they too were now safe. Maybe she had travelled with these people, he suggested. Perhaps she knew them very well and was concerned for their safety if she spoke to the police. Maybe she was terrified of the man who had been shot. He was now being treated under guard in another hospital and facing serious criminal charges. He spoke as slowly and deliberately as he could, and then he sat down again, hoping that he had unlocked the silence.

After another three or four minutes, a man in white medical garb opened the door. He said that was as much questioning as they could permit their patient to undergo. Hennessy heaved a sigh of frustration and slowly stood up, looking at the girl for some sign of response as he and the translator left the room.

At the door, he turned briefly to have one last look at her, but she remained motionless.

Chapter 31

'I hope I'm interrupting a well-deserved romantic interlude with a tall, dark, handsome man, a bottle of wine, and a nice meal?'

'I am in the company of a tall, dark, handsome man, Tim, but I'm afraid you're way off with the context'.

'Ah well, I got one part right AJ'.

'You should be a detective Sergeant Coady'.

'Working on it, AJ; anyway, just called to thank you for coming in early the other night,' said the Sergeant.

'No worries, Tim, hope you're feeling better; you got a bit of a shock tackling those guys at the Cargo Terminal'.

Just as Tim was about to answer, a roar from the engine test cell behind the station made him stop. AJ could hear the distinctive sound from her end of the call and waited for it to end.

'Much better, thank you. Where are you anyway? Can you talk?' said Coady when the noise abated.

'Sure, give me a second,' answered AJ holding the phone while she found some privacy.

'Now I can talk; I was viewing an apartment, and the estate agent was indeed tall, dark and handsome, but it was an open viewing, and half a dozen others were looking at it, mainly couples, so romance certainly wasn't on the agenda' she explained.

'So, you're buying your own place, AJ, good for you,' said a delighted Coady.

'Jesus no, on my salary? My lease runs out in a few weeks, so I'm looking for another place to rent'.

'Ah, I see. Near the airport, I suppose?'

'Not necessarily Tim. Why, do you reckon I'm going to be confined to the airport station for the rest of my career?' said a slightly disgruntled AJ.

'That's not what I mean AJ, I just thought for convenience purposes. You know I rate you highly, and you could be in a much more frontline station, but that's not up to me'. Coady knew the background of all the officers assigned to the airport station. He was aware of AJ coming out on the wrong side of a Garda Siochana Ombudsman

Commission investigation into a missing child case in Limerick. It was headline news at the time.

'Yeah, I know Tim. Anyway, I'd like to be closer to the sea, so I'm looking around Clontarf. Talking of career, Tim, what are your plans? You're far too good to be stuck in a backwater like the airport; you did nothing to deserve such an assignment. I did'.

'Your issues with the powers that be are your business AJ, I'm not getting involved, thank you very much. Actually, I requested the airport. We have young kids, and Jean works full time, so it suits me to be around. Who knows, maybe when the kids are a bit older, I'll ask for a transfer or apply for promotion, but for now, I'm quite content here'.

'Good for you, Tim, so what about all the excitement over the past few days, any updates? You heard that Sandra found the suitcase on CCTV? That girl deserves to be working with the other analyst boffins in Headquarters. She's really good at it,' said AJ.

'Sandra was telling me, and yes, I agree she could be put to better use in HQ, but as you know – '

'I know, I know,' interrupted AJ, 'it's not up to you. She, too, fell foul of the powers that be and must serve out her sentence'.

'Something like that, yeah. Anyhow, I haven't heard anything about the cargo robbery or the suitcase murder; I'm not in those circles, I'm afraid.'

'But what do you think, Tim,' quizzed AJ. 'A murder and an armed robbery within twenty-four hours of each other; that can't be a coincidence; they must be connected?'

'I would have thought so but it seems Hennessy doesn't. Although to be fair to him, he's pursuing the third coincidence: Alfie Tobin arriving on the same day, and he's had some success there. You heard about the shooting and the rescue of the six victims of trafficking?'

'Yeah, I heard, and I know Garoid can join the dots pretty well when he puts his mind to it, but he's just so fucking caught up in the politics of looking good; I can't handle that shit!' said AJ.

'Well, not alone did he free the six victims and arrest the guy that was transporting them; I hear he shot him before he fired at one of the NSU people on the scene. Seems she was pretty shaken up after it,' said Sergeant Tim Coady.

'No, I hadn't heard that, and was our murdered girl part of that group?' asked AJ.

'Couldn't tell you, but I reckon either she was or the girl they arrested in Tobin's house in Balbriggan was, or both of them were too many coincidences'.

The jet engine being tested roared again as Coady finished layout out his hypothesis, so there was a lull in the call while they both waited for it to die down.

After about ten seconds, AJ gave her own thoughts.

'They'll know a lot more when they finish processing the fingerprints and conducting the interviews. However, I'm still confused about the movement of the suitcase. How was that bag moved around secure areas without getting picked up on the cameras? And where was this poor girl actually murdered? Surely it had to be at the airport?'

'So many questions AJ but not for us to answer. Gotta' go, they're inviting me to some of their Royal Visit meetings, not sure why. Best of luck with your apartment search'.

He was right, of course, thought AJ as she headed back in to talk to the estate agent showing the seafront apartment. But I'm not giving up on helping them.

Further than you think

deeper than you sink

higher than you clink

faster than you blink.

How the mighty fall

how the desperate maul

how the innocent bawl

how the guilty crawl

Chapter 32

There were seven messages on Hennessy's phone when he got out into the hospital car park. Three were from DS Brophy, three from his investigation team and one that he prioritised to return the call.

'Calvin, hi, returning your call,' said an expectant Hennessy.

'Yes, Garoid, thanks for getting back to me. I just wanted to let you know that we can confirm the six people from the house in Tallaght were definitely in Alfie Tobin's house in Balbriggan. Also, that Ger Cosgrave was definitely in the Tallaght property but not in the Balbriggan one'.

'Okay, that's very helpful in charging Cosgrave, and what about our murder victim?' asked Hennessy.

'Sorry, there's no evidence of her in either house. That doesn't mean she wasn't there, of course, just that we haven't found any evidence to confirm it,' said Dr Calvin Walshe, trying to lessen the bad news.

'But doesn't any contact leave a trace, Cal? Isn't that your mantra?'

'I know, I know, but maybe it was cleaned after she was murdered?' suggested the forensics expert, without much conviction.

'And you found evidence that cleaning materials had been used to sanitise surfaces?' probed Hennessy.

'Well, no, we haven't specifically identified any deliberate cleansing actions,' said Walshe, sounding like he regretted suggesting it.

'Thanks anyway, Cal, anything else comes up, let me know,' Hennessy was already dialling another number before Walshe had time to reply.

'Jenny, tell me we've found Tobin?' he said before his detective had time to speak.

'Not quite Gar, but we may have identified the apartment he's in. You got my message?'

'Yip, you said it might be one of two?'

'Correct, but since then, I've spoken to Lucas again, and he checked with the girl who said she saw the number on the door and that it was either 66 or 68. She said the window in the living room definitely faced into the courtyard, so that excludes 66 which faces Smithfield Square,' explained Jenny Pilger.

'Okay, Lucas left a message as well about his interviews. Seems only one of the six can speak English or admits to it. Has the warrant arrived?' asked Hennessy.

'Not yet, Gar, but we're told it's on the way. There are five officers on site, but the NSU people are saying they need to move out, so I've asked the Bridewell to get us some people'.

'For fuck's sake, are the NSU too fucking precious to break down a door and arrest a key suspect?' stormed Hennessy, opening the door of his car.

'Sorry Jenny,' he continued before she had said anything, I'm not blaming you, but those fucking prima donnas never want to get their hands dirty!'

'I'm not defending them, Gar, but I think they figure they can't do much undercover surveillance if they're on social media smashing down doors,' suggested Jenny Pilger.

'Right, right,' said Hennessy starting the engine, 'I'm on my way'.

As he pulled out of the hospital car park heading for the city centre, he turned on his blue light and siren and then dialled Detective Wang.

'Wang, look, I got your message, but I'm on the way into town. Can you stay there and keep looking for another hour or two, and we should all be able to meet you there and see where were at?'

'Okay, Sir, will do,' confirmed Wang.

The final call Hennessy wanted to make before he reached the apartment building - Brophy would have to wait until he had something positive to update her on - was to Lucas Hannon but when he rang, the phone was on voicemail.

'Lucas, I got your message, and I'm in a hurry now, so can you finish your interviews and meet me at the airport station in a couple of hours please? Wang is there, and I'll bring Jenny. We need to catch up. Cheers'.

Hennessy was about two miles from the apartment when he switched off the light and siren but didn't reduce his speed.

Chapter 33

Jenny Pilger got out of the black van she was in, crossed the road, and climbed into the passenger side of the light blue sedan.

'We have the warrant. No. 68 is on the third floor, so we go in the pedestrian entrance on this side, leaving one officer beside the car park entrance. They can see the apartment's living room window from there just in case anyone is stupid enough to jump or try to climb down. That leaves us two and two armed detectives from the Bridewell to go in the front door,' explained Pilger, beginning to breathe a little heavier now as the adrenalin kicked in.

'Good work Jenny,' said Hennessy, 'let's go.'

When they got to the pedestrian entrance, Jenny beckoned to two people in civilian clothes sitting in a white SUV across the road from it. The two officers, one male and one female, quickly joined them as Jenny used the key fob she had borrowed from the management company to open the electronic gate.

The four Gardaí hurried along the wall of the block they were entering until they arrived at another security door. When Jenny opened it, she turned to the two officers from the Bridewell station and explained where they were heading. She asked them to take the lift while she and Hennessy used the stairs.

As they were walking up the stairs, Hennessy whispered something that she didn't quite catch.

'What was that?' she asked in a hushed tone.

'I can't go in first,' repeated a slightly embarrassed Hennessy.

Pilger was a little taken aback but didn't want to show it, so she nodded her head in agreement.

When Hennessy saw the look on her face, even though it was momentary, he felt obliged to explain.

'Jenny, I can't go in first because I don't have a firearm'.

Again, Jenny turned to look at him, this time showing a lot more confusion in her expression.

'They took it off me...GSOC....because of the Cosgrave shooting,' he explained.

Jenny indicated she understood as she slowly opened the door onto the third-floor landing.

The two Bridewell officers were standing beside the lift, out of sight of no. 68 when Jenny whispered to draw their weapons. She explained that Hennessy would kick the door in, and she would enter first. After that, they were to remain outside unless there was any shooting or they were called in.

A sense of déjà vu assailed Hennessey as he realised the corridor was similar to the one he'd walked with Anna Jenkinson some years ago looking for a lost girl. He hoped the outcome would be better this time.

As they gently approached the grey door, Jenny withdrew her own Walther P99C. She fought to control her breathing and stop her hand shaking while hoping that the flimsy-looking door hadn't been reinforced in any way.

Chapter 34

The cream cakes in the display cabinet looked too ravishing to resist. Apple slices, jam doughnuts, profiteroles, coffee rolls, the choice was tantalising.

Positioning his tray beside the profiteroles, the smiley-faced man with the gold crucifix earring selected two and continued along the queue to order two coffees.

When he sat at the table beside the cafe's front door, wearing a bright blue blazer and a wide-collared dark orange shirt, he noticed his companion's reaction to the treats on his tray and quickly offered encouragement.

'You know you want one girlfriend; don't give me that diet nonsense. You're looking as fit as a fiddle and lean as a rake!'

'Thanks Dom, and thanks for asking me out for a coffee'.

'You're very welcome, girl; now tell me all about your life?'

'Well, the airport has suddenly gone from Boredsville to crime central so... '

'Not your work-life, Anna Jenkinson, your *luuuuve* life, of course!' interrupted Dominick Rollins, her good friend since their school days.

'If that's what we're going to talk about Dom, this will be a very short chat'.

'Tut, tut, tut, that's not the man-magnet I remember from back in the day, AJ; you must have just lost interest?' asked Dominick, taking a bite from his profiterole.

'Maybe I lost a bit of motivation for a while, but things are looking up. Work is genuinely busy, and I've started looking for a new apartment,' said AJ trying to appear livelier.

'Excellent! You're finally putting a foot on the property ladder. Good for you, girl!'

'Not exactly, Dominick. I'm moving from my one-bed rented apartment to another one-bed rented apartment,' explained AJ.

'Oh' said Dominick, 'well, that's a new start, I guess? Onwards and upwards as they say'.

'Absolutely. But enough about me; tell me what you've been up to? Last time we spoke, there was a new man in your life, a doctor as I recall?' said AJ, happy to change the subject.

As she looked at Dominick, waiting for a response, she noticed the stares he was getting from three schoolboys that had come in and sat opposite them. AJ had heard their high spirits when they were locking up their bikes outside, but she didn't expect this reaction to her flamboyant friend. She saw that Dominick was aware of their attention also as he turned his body so he could face away from them.

'Oh, that ended a good while ago AJ, I'm seeing a Spanish guy for the last few months. He works for one of the IT companies in that Digital Hub near the Guinness Hop Store, and he's really gentle and kind. Probably too gentle and kind to stay with me for long'.

The schoolboys at this stage had started sniggering. One of them was cleaning out his schoolbag on the table and flicking crushed paper pieces onto the floor.

Dominick could see AJ getting a little irritated with them and tried to divert her attention.

'AJ don't worry about it, honestly. It's fine, I'm used to it. Tell me where you're planning to move to?'

AJ slowly responded while still firing dagger looks at the schoolboys.

'Somewhere on the seafront, I'm thinking, maybe Clontarf'.

'There's a lovely promenade in Clontarf, all right. So staying near the airport then?'

'No!' AJ replied a little brusquely, 'you're the second person that said that to me. The airport has nothing to do with it. I'm not planning to stay there for the rest of my career. I just happen to like living closer to the sea'.

Dominick could see that she was getting annoyed and wasn't sure if it was his question or the ongoing comments from the schoolboys that was responsible. He decided a break would be timely, so he excused himself to go to the bathroom.

As he got up, one of the schoolboys whistled at him, and the chorus of sniggering took on a greater intensity. Other diners were turning around now, and the staff member at the cash register was looking over.

'Hey, gorgeous!' the smallest of the three half-stood up from his seat and shouted over to AJ, 'come on over and join us. You won't get much action out of that gayboy!'

Their table erupted with laughter.

AJ was drumming her fingertips on the table and contemplating whether or not she had time to shut the boys up before Dominick got back. She knew he would be upset if he saw her getting embroiled in a row on his behalf.

The girl at the cash register saved her from making the decision by approaching and asking them to behave themselves or leave the cafe. She then turned to AJ and apologised for their behaviour, offering another two coffees on the house through recompense.

'We're good, thank you,' she replied, 'we're just wrapping up, but thanks anyway'.

There was no reaction from their neighbours when Dominick came back and sat down.

'I have an idea Dom; why don't we meet up this weekend for a good old booze-up, like the old days? Unless, of course, you have a heavy date?'

'As it happens, I have! On Friday night, but Saturday works for me,' answered an excited Dominick.

'Saturday it is then. I'll round up a few of the crew. If you're all done, let's go. I need to get a jog in tonight if I'm going to be knocking back shedloads of beer in a few nights!'

On their way out, AJ heard a strange noise coming from the schoolboys' table. She glanced sideways to see one of them sticking two fingers in his mouth and making an obscene gesture in her direction. She kept moving and hoped Dominick didn't see it.

AJ looked along the front of the building as Dominick hugged her outside.

'7pm Saturday in the usual place?' she asked.

'Can't wait!' replied Dominick as he walked away.

When the three schoolboys emerged from the cafe twenty minutes later and discovered their bikes chained together with a heavy-duty lock, AJ was almost home. I'll go past the cafe on my run later on, and maybe I'll remove the chain if it's still there, she thought.

Progress may be measured

in acts and scholarly form

but tolerance is treasured

when no one has to mourn

Chapter 35

The mood was grim when Garoid Hennessy and Jenny Pilger joined their colleagues at the airport station that Wednesday evening. Lucas Hannon and Wang had heard the news from the distillery apartment building and weren't looking forward to this update.

'That useless prick wasn't there!' stormed Hennessy when he shoved open the door of the meeting room.

'After all that, Tobin managed to get out, thanks to our fucking useless NSU who couldn't monitor a fucking bull in a fucking china shop!'

'Do we know how or when?' ventured Hannon trying not to show his discomfort.

'We think he skedaddled when he heard that Cosgrave got shot and the victims rescued. NSU figures he merged with the dozens of people leaving for work. It was raining, so everyone had umbrellas and coats and hats and hoodies; they couldn't watch them all', answered Jenny Pilger to let her boss calm down.

'So, we don't know if it was on foot or car?' probed Hannon, hoping he wouldn't get pilloried by Hennessy for asking a stupid question.

'Nope,' confirmed Pilger, 'forensics are there now and we're checking the CCTV in the building but I wouldn't be confident'.

'So, it was completely empty?' asked Wang.

'Completely' butted in Hennessy, 'so hopefully, we get fingerprints putting Tobin, Cosgrave, the six victims, and if we're really lucky, the murder victim there'.

'It looked like it had been left in a hurry,' added Jenny Pilger, 'and there was no smell of disinfectant so we're reasonably confident of finding trace evidence'.

'So let's see where we're at then,' sighed Hennessy rubbing his eyes with the back of his hand, 'we've got an unidentified girl who was brutally murdered, an officer out of surgery but still badly injured, an Asian girl also injured and refusing to say anything, a suspect with gunshot wounds under armed guard in hospital, six victims who are being interviewed without much success, and a chief suspect we can't find'.

He looked at Lucas Hannon first for an update.

'I've been interviewing the six people we picked up in Tallaght,' Hannon explained, 'and only one of them is saying anything. She was the one who gave us the apartment number but she won't tell us where they're from or how they got here. It looks like they've been told to say nothing, or they would suffer for it. They're all petrified, and the translators couldn't get a beep out of them. Their best bet is a mixture of Vietnamese and Chinese citizens, ranging from the mid-20s to mid-40s. They had no papers whatsoever with them. When I showed them photos of Cosgrave, Tobin, etc., there was no particular reaction. There are three Immigration officers with them now trying to figure them out'.

Hennessy stepped in again: 'Calvin Walshe confirmed earlier that they were in Tobin's place in Balbriggan and that Cosgrave's prints were found in Tallaght but still nothing on the murder victim. That gives us strong evidence to charge Cosgrave with trafficking, etc., but we still need to prove Tobin was in the Tallaght house or the city centre apartment; his prints are all over the Balbriggan house but he lives there, so that's hardly earth shattering'.

'But that still only gets bringing trafficking charges against Tobin; it doesn't link him to the murder victim', said Hannon, pointing out the obvious.

'I fucking know that Hannon!' snarled Hennessy, 'which is probably why my boss is chasing me all day to see if we're investigating a human smuggling ring or a murder, and I have no doubt she'll say that such a quandary is discombobulating her!'

He turned to Wang and nodded at him to speak.

'I've been following up the suitcase that Sandra here in the station found on the CCTV footage. It appears on a trolley in the baggage hall, and it looks very much like the one our murdered girl was found in, but there are blind spots that hinder us following the bag's movements,' said Wang as he opened up his laptop and tapped on a few keys.

'So, nothing new?' sighed Hennessy.

'Not necessarily,' replied Wang 'we have picked up a shadow close to the bag that appears in one image when the bag is on the trolley and another when the bag is gone. It looks like the same shadow of a person in a bulky jacket or overalls, but it's pretty fuzzy. We're following it up, but Sandra finished her shift an hour ago, and my eyes are as wonky from hours of squinting at the footage as hers were. We're going to pick it up again in the morning and take a tour of the area if that's okay with you?' he added, looking at Hennessy.

'Absolutely, let me know if you need more resources,' replied Hennessy with a bit more enthusiasm than his previous comments.

'So forensics from the apartment, interviews with the six trafficked people, following up with Wang's shadow, and finding Tobin; is that where we're at?' asked Jenny Pilger, attempting to summarise and conclude the meeting, and go home before she fell asleep at her desk.

'That's about it,' confirmed Hennessy. 'Thanks, folks, I appreciate the effort. I'll brief DS Brophy, and we'll talk tomorrow. I'm hoping to get to interview that bollocks Cosgrave then.'

Chapter 36

The Aer Lingus flight from New York's Kennedy airport arrived ten minutes early into Dublin.

Fifty minutes after landing, the passengers had cleared Immigration, collected their bags, and filed out to the Arrivals Floor. Limousine drivers and tour operators jostled for position with their welcome signs held out displaying passenger and group names. Public announcements were no longer made to connect people since the airport adopted a 'reduced noise' policy.

One of the passengers ignored the meeters and greeters and followed the Food Court signs until he found the Grill Bar. He was six foot three inches tall, slim in a dark grey designer suit and wearing black leather brogues. He walked down the aisle on the left-hand side and slid into the end booth, parking his navy wheelie suitcase adjacent to the seat.

'How was your flight?' asked Florin Ardelean

'Punctual,' replied Rod Whitney, making himself comfortable.

'You don't have a deep south accent Mr Whitney?' enquired Florin.

'How did you know where I'm from?'

'I make it a point to research my collaborators, Mr Whitney, particularly ones I am paying a great deal of money to'.

'Well, I'm not sure that Chapel Hill is considered the Deep South strictly speaking. Besides, I spent most of my adult life in Washington, but I presume you know that?'

'I know you spent several years as a guest of the United States Government, Mr Whitney,' said Florin pointedly as he watched a group of four travellers with a trolley of baggage sitting into a booth mid-way down the same aisle.

'Affirmative, but you still hired me. By the way, they call me Nacie, N-A-C-I-E,' he spelt out.

'Nacie? When your first name is Rodney?' asked Florin.

'Long story. Folk in Washington first referred to me as NC', as in North Carolina, which morphed into Nacie over the years. Not really sure how'.

'I'm not sure an explanation is necessary but might I suggest we order some breakfast and then discuss business?' suggested Florin, picking up the plastic menu.

Chapter 37

Thank heavens Brophy's phone was on voicemail last night Detective Inspector Garoid Hennessy thought as he parked in the reserved area in front of Tallaght University Hospital. He knew that the update message he left wouldn't keep her happy for long so he would have to arrange a meeting with her later.

The armed officer on the fourth-floor landing recognised him and opened the door into the room beside the nurse's station. The blinds on the window were half-drawn, and the occupant was lying on his side facing the window. His shoulder was heavily strapped, and his hand was in a sling.

'Good morning Mr Cosgrave, and how are you today?' asked Hennessy as if he cared.

Cosgrave's startled reaction was followed quickly by a grimace as he turned on to his back and felt his injuries kick in.

'I'm suing you. You tried to fucking kill me, you dirty bastard!' said Cosgrave with venom.

'I wish I had killed you, you useless good-for-nothing prick; I was aiming for your head'.

'Fuck off away from me; I'm in recovery. I'm not talking to anyone without my solicitor,' shouted Cosgrave.

'Look, Cosgrave, you're already under caution and about to be charged with attempting to shoot a member of An Garda Siochana, human trafficking, kidnapping and a shitload of other crimes, so you're not going to be breathing fresh air for a fucking long time'.

Cosgrave didn't answer but stared menacingly at the Detective Inspector.

'This isn't a formal interview', Hennessy went on; 'it's to find out if you have any useful information for my murder inquiry. If you have, it could benefit you in dealing with the courts?'

Still no response from Cosgrave.

Hennessy wasn't giving up.

'Look, Cosgrave, they've given me half an hour because you're in *such poor health,* and personally, I hope you spend the rest of your miserable fucking life in prison, but you can do yourself a big favour here by helping out'.

As he finished the sentence, Hennessy took out his notebook and pretended to flick through the pages, a bit like a student when the teacher is picking someone in class to answer a question.

The Detective knew the routine by now from his training and his experience: allow the import of what you've said to sink in and let him think you're distracted by something else.

Another two minutes ticked by; the flickers of sunlight breaking through the window blinds gave way to the gloominess of the dark clouds looming outside, with their ever-present threat of rain.

Time for the next phase in the process, thought Hennessy.

'So as of now in case you're wondering, cos I can hear the wheels turning from here and I know muscles-for-hire scumbags like you are thick as two short planks, we have eight witnesses – four Guards and four civilians – who saw you point a loaded revolver at a Garda. We have your fingerprints in the house in Tallaght where we found six victims of human trafficking, and we're about to confirm your prints in the city centre apartment that we followed you from with the six victims. That's what, fifteen to twenty years? You know the sentencing system better than any of us.'

Hennessy was warming up nicely now. For some reason, he recalled that the training session in Templemore Training College on this particular interview situation had Anna Jenkinson playing the role of the suspect.

Not that he could compare the intellect of AJ with the sack of shit lying in front of him.

But of course, Cosgrave knew the routine as well; he had been around the block, spending many years behind bars.

Hennessy could only hope that the medication was dulling whatever minuscule amount of brainpower this cretin possessed.

'I notice your solicitor isn't Tobin's, so your boss doesn't give a flying fuck how bad it goes for you either.

And we know Tobin is behind this, and when we pick him up, your bargaining power goes the way of your useless life...down the fucking swanny!'

Hennessy went back to his notes, now deliberately not making eye contact with Cosgrave and knowing that visiting time and interview stages were going against him. Hennessy took out his pen, wrote something slightly exaggerated, and then put pen and notebook back into his inside jacket pocket.

The idea was to give the impression that he'd wrapped up the interview, and the suspect had blown his chance of any kind of reprieve, no matter how small it might be.

Hennessy took out his mobile phone as if he were checking for messages before moving on to his next task.

As he read the same texts and emails that he had already checked coming in from the car, it struck him that Cosgrave might be staying schtum because he didn't actually know anything that could be of assistance to the suitcase murder. Or maybe he's simply scared of what Tobin and his likes have done to other people who crossed them.

Even if he didn't know anything about the murder, surely he'd pretend that he did, just to get some leverage with the charges he was facing, thought the Detective Inspector.

Then again, what if Tobin and Cosgrave weren't directly involved in the murder? That thought left Hennessy with a cold shiver down his back. There was a good chance that they knew something about it, given their career choices and the types of people they associated with.

'Okay, I'm done,' Hennessey concluded as he stood up suddenly and aggressively from his chair, 'you can fuck off and die roaring Cosgrave'.

These hospital interviews were getting him nowhere in this case, thought Hennessy as he opened the door and prepared to instruct his colleague outside to put the suspect in handcuffs, hospital bed or no hospital bed.

His train of thought was interrupted by a voice behind him.

'What if I did know something? What are you offering, Hennessy?'

Chapter 38

A white image of the moon adorned the back of the black hoodie worn by the man leaning on the railing near the coffee kiosk on Dublin's boardwalk. His hood covered half his face, and he had been standing there for over an hour. Every few minutes, he would half turn and observe the other boardwalk users, a mixture of tourists, locals, and drug users.

It was sunny but cold with a biting sharpness to the wind blowing up the river Liffey.

After another hour of pretending to look into the river, periodically checking the pedestrians in the area, the man decided the wind was too cold, and he was too exposed, to prolong his search.

Walking back towards O'Connell Street, he noticed two men having a heated conversation outside a coffee shop further up the road. He slowed down and continued to observe them discretely while crossing over to that side of the road.

He stopped in front of a small antique shop with a dusty old gramophone in the window when he got within about thirty metres of the two quarrelling individuals. The passers-by kept him reasonably hidden had either one looked in his direction.

Less than a minute later, he saw one of the men point his finger aggressively at the other, accompanied by angry words. Then the man stalked across the road towards the river.

The other man turned down a laneway that linked the quays with a busy shopping street. The observer hurried away from his position at the antique shop and followed the man into the laneway. He'd finally caught up with the person he had spent most of the day looking for; a man who got his nickname from his primary school English teacher's request to spell 'dagger'.

He checked behind him and then grabbed the shorter but heavier man by the neck of his denim jacket and hauled him to the ground.

'Digger, you inbred bollox, I've been looking for you!' snarled Alfie Tobin as he brought his knee into the neck and jaw of Paul 'Digger' Flood with as much force as he could generate.

Digger looked up in surprise and terror as his head and right shoulder hit the wall. Tobin heard a crack as something broke in Digger, and the man cried out in pain and clutched his head. Digger opened his mouth as if to speak, but Tobin's right fist, with its chunky gold ring, caught him in the eye and pushed his head into the wall again.

This time the injured man stayed quiet and still, but Tobin wasn't finished.

'I gave you one simple job, one basic fucking task: to transport merchandise from point A to point B, something that a fucking monkey could do, and you fucking mess it up! You left me short, and then you go into fucking hiding! What did you think? That I'd *forget*, you fucking dim-wit?'

There was spit coming from Tobin's mouth as he finished the sentence, and he reinforced his disappointment with another fist to Digger's face, lower down this time, catching the cheek and nose. Again, Digger's head hit the wall.

Digger's cropped blond hair had blood in it from somewhere, and the left side of his face looked like a shish kebab that had been driven over by an articulated truck.

His eye was closing over, and blood from his broken nose flowed liberally down his denim jacket and black AC/DC t-shirt. He blurted out a defence.

'I did exactly what you asked Alfie...I swear on me ma's grave I did!'

The words came out with a slight lisp as his jaw was swelling up, and blood filled his mouth.

Tobin grabbed the collar of Digger's jacket with both hands and lifted his head a few inches off the ground. Then he leaned closer to him and stared into his one open eye.

'You're a lying bastard, Flood, but that's the last lie you'll tell,' he said slowly and with maximum menace.

Tobin's right hand reached into his jeans pocket. The expression on Digger's face told Tobin the man knew that the flick-knife was coming out, and that meant Digger's life expectancy was down to minutes.

'Tell me what I did wrong, Alfie, for fuck's sake?'

Tobin needed to recheck both sides of the laneway before he finished this scumbag off. As he did so, he spelled it out.

'Seven items of merchandise from point A to point B, but you decide six would be enough, and then you lose the seventh, you useless – '

'I didn't short-change you, Alfie,' Digger interrupted as Tobin brought his hand out of his pocket, 'you told me to leave one locked in the house!'

Tobin looked startled; he continued to stare at Digger while he thought about it.

Seeing his chance, Digger continued...

'If I was going to keep one Alfie, why would I leave her in your house?' he pleaded, 'I know I'm not that smart, but I'm not *that* fucking stupid Alfie'.

'But I never told you to leave one,' said Tobin, familiar with the lies people told when they were waiting for a knife to be produced.

'Cosgrave said you wanted the little Vietnamese bitch left in the house, Alfie. I was tying her up when I got the call that the cops were on the way. I swear Alfie, that's what happened. Why else would I leave her?'

Digger's voice was beginning to weaken, and his head lolled to one side. His one good eye seemed to roll back in his head, and his upper body shook violently. Tobin took his hand away from his pocket, and with a quick glance behind him, he took off for the anonymity of the busy street.

Chapter 39

When Hennessy rang his boss to organise an update session, she told him to meet her at the airport after her Royal visit briefing.

He was about to conclude an update with his own team when Brophy texted him to meet her in the conference room in the Garda Station in fifteen minutes.

He stopped for a moment in the car park to gather his thoughts but the cacophony caused by towing vehicles transporting a large aircraft from the maintenance hangar to the parking area on the north apron made thinking impossible.

Inside the station, Sergeant Coady talked to Morris Owens beside the coffee machine. Two senior officers from the Garda National Crime and Security Intelligence Service were conversing near the front window.

DS Brophy was the only one remaining in the conference room.

'I've made a lot of progress since we spoke – '

'Personal pronoun, nominative case, first-person plural Detective Inspector' interrupted Detective Superintendent Marie Brophy.

'Excuse me, ma'am?' asked a confused Hennessy.

'Don't you mean 'we' Detective Inspector; aren't you in charge of a murder investigation *team*?'

'Of course, ma'am, the team has been making good progress since I last updated you. Firstly, forensics has confirmed that the six victims of human smuggling were in Tobin's house in Balbriggan, the city centre apartment, and the house in Tallaght where we found them, AND,' he said with emphasis, 'Tobin's prints have been found in the apartment; he must have left in a hurry. We are continuing to interview the six victims, and so far, one young lady is cooperating. In fact, she provided us with crucial information in identifying the particular apartment number which we raided'.

'That's good news on Tobin, so the other five are refusing to cooperate?' asked Brophy.

'They're either too frightened to speak, or they don't have sufficient English. We're using our official translator service to help us find out which'.

'And your hope is that they know the murder victim, I presume?'

'Absolutely, ma'am. I believe that it's too big a coincidence if they don't. On that point ma'am, I interviewed the girl we arrested in Balbriggan, the one who assaulted our officer, but I'm afraid she wasn't prepared or able to cooperate. However, I'm convinced that I can get her to help us, so I will try again as soon as the medics approve access'.

'Congeries of leads so far Garoid that aren't helping us with the inquiry so – '

'I haven't finished updating you, ma'am,' interrupted Hennessy before Brophy could rebuke him.

'We believe that we've identified a person of interest in the form of a shadow picked up on CCTV footage near the suitcase in the airport baggage hall. My team has walked the ground to take measurements. Our technical people in HQ are working hard on better images and dimensions such as height, direction, etc. As this is a secure area ma'am, we are hopeful that we can get a name promptly if we can compile a clearer profile'.

Hennessy could see that Brophy still wasn't that impressed, so he wasted no time in unleashing his trump card, hoping that his strategy of keeping the best until last would pay off.

'But the most crucial development, ma'am, is Cosgrave's agreement to cooperate with us'.

'My auricular senses are awoken, Garoid,' said Brophy, 'please continue your accretion.'

Not entirely sure what the big words meant, Hennessy quickly resumed. 'Well, Cosgrave is still in hospital recovering from his gunshot wound, ma'am – '

'An injury administered by your good self Garoid.' cut in Brophy.

'Correct, ma'am. I was granted half an hour with him by his medical team, and he has agreed to talk if it benefits him. I've informed him, of course, that it depends on what information he can give us, and I specifically pointed out that the murder investigation is my primary interest'.

'That's quite interesting, Detective, particularly given this man's employers, dirty bastarding reprobates all. Ocularity may be emerging, a reckoning for dubiety,' said Brophy.

'Sorry, ma'am?' asked a confused Hennessy, quite convinced that his boss didn't fully understand the words she was using either.

'A clearer fucking picture, Detective!' explained Brophy emphatically yet unconvincingly.

'Yes, ma'am. Tobin's solicitor didn't turn up to brief him, so I took that as an opportunity to tell him they were throwing him under the bus. When that sank in, he decided he'd take his chances with a deal. I've asked our legal people to take a statement under oath to see what he has to offer; that should be happening any time now'.

'Felicitations Garoid. That could be just the breakthrough we need. And you still believe that that heinous bollox Tobin will feature protuberantly in the poor girl's demise?'

Hennessy was nodding affirmatively when he saw a text appear on his phone beside the paperwork spread across the table in front of him. It was from the hospital, and his heart sank when he read it.

Tobin's solicitor has turned up to sit in on the interview with Cosgrave!

Chapter 40

AJ was eating a homemade chicken and bacon pizza in her kitchen before getting ready for a night shift when her phone rang.

She recognised the number of the estate agent that had shown her the apartment in Clontarf, and her expectations rose.

'Hi, is that Ms Jenkinson? It's Aonghus here from Baxter Neville; I showed you the apartment in The Cloisters?'

AJ feigned a slight surprise before answering, not wishing to show her interest.

'Eh...the one overlooking the seafront, was it?'

'Yes, that's the one'.

'Right yes, yes I remember now. Thanks for ringing me back,' she said, trying to play it cool.

'So, we had huge interest, and I've discussed the applicants with the owner of the apartment and... I'm afraid we won't be offering you this particular property on this occasion, Ms Jenkinson. However, I do have several similar properties coming on the market shortly, and I'm sure you'll find they suit your needs,' said Aonghus attempting to let her down gently and retain a potential customer.

'I see, and they overlook the seafront?' asked AJ hopefully.

'Well, not quite,' replied Aonghus, 'but within a few minutes on foot or by car'. AJ knew that was real estate speak for: *if you're an Olympic sprinter or Formula 1 driver.*

'Maybe get back to me when you have something along the seafront, please, and thanks for letting me know,' said AJ briskly, making sure her disappointment was evident.

At all costs to be winning

all the heads to be spinning

at all times to be grinning

'The smell'.

'I beg your pardon?' responded AJ as she entered the station to start her shift on Thursday night.

'The smell,' repeated Sandra Whelan with her eyes focused intently on her computer screen.

'You really do know how to make friends and influence people, Sandra, I'll give you that'.

Sandra shook her head impatiently.

'No, there's something odd here. The Duty Cleaning Supervisor got a call reporting a smell in the baggage reclaim hall and tasked one of the staff to follow up, yes?' asked Sandra.

'That's correct, Sandra,' confirmed AJ showing more interest now.

'But dead bodies don't start to smell for several days, under normal circumstances, and the post-mortem indicates that she was killed within twelve hours of discovery'.

'Unless, of course, the victim emptied their bowel and bladder contents at the time of death,' said AJ picking up the logic, 'and that wasn't apparent when I opened the suitcase'.

'Or in the post-mortem,' continued Sandra.

'Which means that......?' went on AJ, handing back to her colleague.

'The person making the call was involved'.

'Or the person taking the call was involved,' added AJ, with her theory of staff involvement coming to the fore again.

'Good work, Sandra, but surely the investigation team copped that?'

'It's not in any of their reports that I can access online, and I've spent the last day going through CCTV tapes with Wang, and he didn't mention it,' said Sandra.

'We did a long walkabout following up this shadow and took all kinds of measurements for the HQ boffins,' she went on as she tidied her desk at the end of her shift.

'I got your email on that Sandra, thanks for keeping me in the loop. So did you mention the smell thing to Wang?' asked AJ, without dwelling on the irony of Sandra Whelan calling someone else a boffin.

'Thought I'd let you mention it to Hennessy?' said Sandra figuring that it might get AJ closer to the investigation, whatever about closer to Hennessy.

'I might say it to him tomorrow; I'm going to do my patrol now'.

Chapter 41

On his drive home from the airport, Hennessy cursed Tobin's cursed intervention in his breakthrough in getting Cosgrave to talk. But, at the same time, he was pleased that it went some way to confirming Tobin's involvement in the murder.

He wondered how Tobin would have known that they had Cosgrave by the short and curlies for the smuggling and firearms charges. Why would he send his solicitor unless it was to protect Cosgrave against more serious charges?

There again, how come he hadn't sent his solicitor to the earlier interview if that was the case, he pondered and then groaned as he thought about how Brophy would react when she got the news that the deal had fallen through. The call came from the legal eagles as he was working through these scenarios.

'So he bottled it and gave us nothing?' said Hennessy when he answered the call.

'Pretty much,' responded Emer Dockery from the legal team assigned to the case.

'He didn't mention Tobin once and claimed he never gave you any such indication,' she went on.

'And the human smuggling and firearms charges?'

'You'll love this Detective. He claims that the six people in the house asked him to transport them and were looking for asylum, not being smuggled. He hadn't hurt or threatened any of them, he claims. He was merely – wait for it - making a humanitarian gesture'.

Hennessy was annoyed but not that surprised. He had heard such defences before.

'And the firearms charges? Don't tell me: it wasn't his gun and he thought we were robbers, so he had to defend himself'.

'Close Detective. He says you didn't identify yourselves as Gardaí, and he was told a local gang was planning to kidnap the six individuals to use them for illegal purposes'.

'Figures, anyway thanks for the help Emer; enjoy your evening'.

'One other thing, Detective. He says he's going to sue you personally for *maiming* him. Claims he'll be disabled for the rest of his life due to you shooting him, and he'll be looking for compensation for pain, trauma, stress, lost earnings, blah, blah, blah..'.

'Thanks, Emer, good night!' said a smiling Hennessy as he thought that next time, he would shoot the bastard in the fucking head.

Chapter 42

Shadows and staff members

suitcases and smells

the answer is devious

whatever it tells

When AJ had finished walking around the multi-storey car parks, the cargo area, and the airline office buildings, she made her way into the arrivals level of the passenger terminal.

The activity level had increased as the weekend drew closer, and a big rugby game in the Capital saw an influx of European visitors.

In the baggage sorting hall, she spent time figuring out where the shadow had appeared and how easy or difficult it might have been to avoid the cameras.

The baggage dollies in the transit area had several ski and golf bags protruding from under the canvas covers while the reclaim belts were being used by four different flights, according to the monitors above them.

She counted a dozen ground handling staff coming and going as she scrutinised the shadows those on foot were casting against the brick walls and concrete floor. They reminded her of the House of Mirrors attraction at the Malahide festival she attended every year with her school pals. Depending on your location and which direction you were facing or moving, relative to the high-intensity discharge lights in the ceiling, there seemed to be an almost infinite variety of shadows. Identifying an individual from the shadow Sandra and Wang picked up was a difficult task. Still, she assumed the technical people knew what they were doing.

She was more interested in how someone could move in and out of the transit baggage area without being captured by the CCTV system.

As she strolled between the dollies, tracking the two fixed cameras that could pick up parts of that zone, it struck her there appeared to be a blind spot between the back wall and belt number seven that might just allow someone to get in and out without being caught on camera.

She would need to check with Sandra to see precisely what size images the cameras were recording, but even if a human could avoid them, how could they possibly bring the suitcase with them? And how could they follow such a crooked and unusual path without other staff noticing it, particularly on a busy Sunday afternoon shift?

These questions and more were occupying AJ's mind when she was interrupted by someone approaching her from the other side of the hall.

'Good evening officer, anything I can help you with?'

'I'm good, thanks Tony, just double-checking something,' she answered Tony Gibbons, the ground handling shift supervisor. His demeanour was intrusive, which immediately made AJ clam up.

'There were a few of your people over here looking at the same spot earlier I hear; something to do with the girl in the suitcase, I presume?'

'As I said, Tony, just checking something. Hope I wasn't interfering with the operation,' said AJ as she moved away, not inclined to furnish Gibbons with any details.

'Fair enough, Officer Jenkinson, just trying to help'.

Mirrors that deceive

outlines changing hue

wondering who to believe

what may be false or true.

A breath away from a breakthrough

a chasm away from an arrest

a leaning towards an individual

a fear of failing the test

When AJ arrived back at the station, she took the squad car keys off their hook and drove onto the airside through the cargo vehicle access post. She was looking for something in particular.

Chapter 43

Conscious of the cameras at the vehicle entrance, Florin Ardelean picked up Nacie Whitney down the road from his hotel early on Friday morning. Nacie was wheeling one of the suitcases that he had brought with him.

They drove in silence, Ardelean checking his rear-view mirror regularly, along the boundary of the Curragh racecourse for the short time it took to reach the warehouse Ardelean rented for his import/export business. The fewer questions asked about the nature of the goods he was importing and exporting, the better it suited Ardelean.

When the creaky warehouse door closed behind them, Ardelean and Whitney got out of the vehicle. They walked over to the horsebox containing two wooden crates.

'We haven't opened them,' said Ardelean by way of prompting Whitney to say something.

'Good,' said Whitney, 'some of the parts are solid, but some are quite sensitive'.

'So how long to get it assembled?'

'Assuming everything is here and undamaged, a day or so,' replied Whitney.

With Ardelean leaving to attend to other business, Whitney set about the task at hand.

First, he cleared away the boxes and the litter from the corner of the warehouse furthest away from the vehicle entrance. Next, he stuck black plastic sheeting around the two windows at ground level. Finally, he brushed the cleared area that measured about four metres square, waited a few minutes for the dust to settle, and laid out three long strips of brown craft paper on the floor. The final piece of the preparation area was a wooden pallet, also specified in advance, measuring 150 cm square and 15 cm high, which he put on top of the paper strips.

Now he was ready to unpack the two wooden crates.

Using a long screwdriver, he gently prised open the lid of each crate, taking care not to create any sudden movement. When he looked inside, the metal was dull and crudely cut with sharp corners and several uneven parts; clear signs he thought that the equipment had originated in Eastern Europe.

However, he was pleased to see that the holding bars were in position. After taking out some cardboard padding, he was able to access and unhook the small toolkit inside. Next, he loosened and removed the four 6 cm metal bars holding the units in place using a small spanner.

Gently lowering one crate at a time so that they were facing each other, he was able to slide out the contents onto the wooden pallet.

Nacie stepped back and had a good look around the two units, smiling to himself as he could see what Ardelean meant when he said that the functional, unexciting look should not distract from some very sophisticated engineering.

Chapter 44

AJ was sitting at her desk with several lever arch folders open in front of her when Sergeant Tim Coady arrived in to start his shift.

There were two frustrated looking passengers standing at the public counter with a lot of documents, but when Coady asked if he could help them, they told him that they were being looked after and thanked him for asking.

AJ looked over and said good morning but quickly reverted to studying the manuals and typing on her computer.

'You look busy, AJ; I don't see those folders being used very often,' said Coady, noticing the Airport Policy folders on her desk. Stored on a bookshelf in the corner of the station and mainly used to explain what happens when cars are clamped or stolen, the staff knew the central policies so well they rarely needed to consult them.

'Did you know Tim that about 0.5% of all checked-in bags around the world are lost? That's about one per 220 bags, which is equivalent to one on every international flight.

'I did not know that AJ, but I do know that it's the air carrier's responsibility to reunite passengers with their luggage, and the most they can claim is Eur1100 regardless of the value of the contents. And I know that the European Court of Justice made that determination based on the Montreal Convention, which was adopted by the European Union in 2001' said a smiling Coady.

'Wow, you're not just a pretty face, huh, Sarg?'

'It's amazing how much you learn when an angry Argentinian gentleman arrives in the middle of the night demanding that I arrest the captain of a long-haul flight from the Middle East because a suitcase containing a handmade Ethiopian grass skirt went missing!'

'Now you know why I never check-in my handmade Ethiopian grass skirts,' said AJ with a smile breaking out.

'But did you also know' she went on, 'that about 200,000 bags are lost every month in the US and that about 0.03% of checked luggage is never reunited with its owner and that most US airlines sell those bags to a big company in Alabama after holding on to them for ninety days? And then they auction them off. There's even a TV reality series about it'.

'I'll be sure and tell the next angry Argentinian passenger exactly that!' replied Coady.

'Irish air carriers have an excellent record both for not losing bags – only about one per 1000 – and of finding them again if they do lose them. They give any unclaimed bags to charities, who can sell on the cases and their contents'.

'That does ring a bell actually,' said Coady, 'not the statistics but the carriers donating the bags to charity, who then sell on any valuable contents'.

When he noticed that AJ had gone back to typing and studying, he restarted the conversation.

'And this is essential information for an airport-based Garda who has just finished a night shift because...?'

When AJ looked up sheepishly, he went on.

'Don't tell me. The girl in the suitcase or girl on the belt, or whatever the media is calling the case these days?'

'Sandra and Detective Sergeant Wang are following up the shadow that they found on the footage in the area. Sandra also informed me about the anomaly of the smell that was initially reported. Anyway, I took a long walk around the baggage sorting hall and started thinking about where the suitcase actually came from. Was it owned by the perpetrators? Was it grabbed from a baggage dolly and the contents binned somewhere? Why hasn't it been reported missing by anyone? Or at least as far as we know it hasn't? That brought me to look at the unclaimed luggage policies of the airlines and the airport authority in more detail. That's why all the files are out, and I'm making calls to some of the lost bag offices,' concluded AJ.

Coady was about to tell her that she could get herself and Sandra into trouble investigating a case they were not assigned to when AJ stepped in again.

'Before you tell me that we have nothing to do with the case, Tim, Sandra was asked to help Wang with the CCTV footage, and Sandra simply asked me to assist. Just on that, it's difficult to tell exactly how much the cameras pick up, so I'm going to go over some of the images with Sandra when she gets in'.

'Fair enough AJ, so long as you're not neglecting your duties around here, that's fine with me. Oh, and don't think you're getting overtime for staying back after your shift!' replied a smiling Coady.

As he was about to say something else, the officer staffing the public counter called him over about a call he just took.

When Hennessy and AJ arrived at the apartment building off O'Connell in Limerick city centre where Matusz was believed to be living and where Zuzanna might now be, they parked their unmarked car on the next street over to approach discretely.

No vehicle was registered to Matusz, but he was known to borrow vans and jeeps from people he hung around with in the construction industry.

They sat in the car for a few minutes to check the area for potential vehicles and establish if they had attracted any undue attention.

Both officers had experience visiting this development to serve warrants and search apartments for contraband, constantly receiving a hostile reception.

They made a final check with Control for updates. They studied the photograph of Matusz supplied by Maja before exiting the car and making their way to apartment number 404 on the fourth floor.

Taking the stairs, they had reached the third-floor landing when they saw two hoodie-clad individuals sprinting up the stairs ahead of them, making expletive-filled comments, the specifics of which they couldn't quite decipher.

Hennessy turned to Jenkinson and suggested in hushed tones that they might be better off waiting for backup. There were too many exits for two officers to cover, and their presence might now have been communicated around the building.

'We don't have time, Gar! This is a CRI case now, and every minute might be crucial,' whispered AJ in response.

Garoid Hennessy sighed and continued up the stairs, more cautiously now.

Looking through the small window in the fire door on the fourth-floor landing to check it was clear, they both nodded in agreement and inched it open before stepping out and listening for any activity.

The emergency lighting was immediately supplemented by another four or five ceiling lights as the motion sensors picked up their movement. They stood slightly hunched to keep below the level of the spy holes in the apartment doors.

Both officers felt uncomfortable in a silence that seemed hostile to them. Hennessy kept his right hand inside his jacket beside his holster, ready to produce it at a moment's notice.

Number 404 was the third unit on the right along the corridor, and they had to pass five other apartments before they got to it.

As they took up positions on either side of the light grey door, there was a sudden burst of activity behind Hennessy. Someone came bolting out of one of the other apartments and shouldered the Emergency Exit door open, racing down the stairs.

'That's him,' shouted AJ, 'Go!' Go!' as she took off after him.

Hennessy didn't get a clear look at the fleeing figure but quickly took off after AJ.

They could hear the footsteps ahead of them as they rushed down the stairs, but all was quiet when they got out of the building and into the poorly lit car park.

The two officers were still breathing heavily from the descent as they slowly checked the parked cars and kept their eyes and ears primed for any movement.

AJ noticed that Hennessy had his gun drawn and whispered sternly that they had no information that the suspect was armed and that he should re-holster it.

They saw green and black industrial bins at the end of the car park with several chairs, and a mattress was thrown up against one of them.

As she got closer, AJ signalled to Hennessy that he should approach them from the other side. As she did, a *car engine started, and a small silver Ford with no lights on shot out of its parking space, heading straight for her.*

'Anyone at home, hello?' asked Sandra Whelan as she walked into the airport station to start her shift.

'Sorry Sandra, I was miles away,' answered AJ, 'can I talk to you about the cameras in the baggage sorting hall, please? I did a walkabout, and I'm trying to figure out how much the cameras pick up'.

'Sure. Did you tell Hennessy about the smell thing?'

'Not yet. I might have a bit more to talk to him about soon,' said AJ.

A small chink of light

a fragile sliver of hope

a view might be in sight

a loosening of the rope

Chapter 45

Holding the update meeting with the team at the airport station was at Wang's request so that the images of the shadow in the baggage sorting office could be fully explained and discussed. Hennessy had seen AJ talking to another officer when he entered the station and nodded a rather chilly greeting to both. He was hoping the meeting would lighten his mood as he took papers out of a two-ringed binder, eyes lingering briefly on the small dark brown mole on his right wrist, and waited for Wang, Lucas Hannon, and Jenny Pilger to get settled around the conference table.

Wang had connected his laptop to the projector screen on the wall, so Hennessy beckoned him to kick things off.

'So, Sandra, from the station here, and I have followed up on this shadow,' Wang held a red dot over the dark image in the corner of the screen.

'We see it when the suitcase – which we're almost certain is the right one – was visible on the dolly, and here again, seventeen minutes later, after the case disappeared even though the dolly it was on is still present.'

Wang moved the recording forward, showing the times and the suitcase in the same montage.

'We can't get a better image than this, and we can't follow the individual on any of the other cameras, which suggests that they are familiar with the CCTV system. Happy to walk the ground again if any of you are interested?' as he looked around the table, but there were no takers.

'So, if this person doesn't have a suitcase in either image, what is their connection to the investigation at all?'

'Well,' he quickly continued before anyone could interject, 'watch this,' as he played footage of a seemingly random selection of vehicles pulling dollies into and out of the hall.

'We counted five separate convoys of baggage during the period in question, three inbound and two outbound. Individual bags are never rolled in or out by hand. However, occasionally, you might see a few stray ones being pushed in on a passenger trolley. Often, they've fallen off the dollies in transit. So, what we're surmising is that someone deliberately moved our suitcase onto one of the convoys, making sure not to be picked up by the cameras while doing so'.

'Why by convoy, why not on to one of the baggage belts?' asked Hennessy.

'Because we can't find it on either the incoming or outgoing baggage belts during this time,' answered Wang.

'The camera coverage of the belts, both here in the sorting hall, for authorised staff only, and in the Reclaim Hall, where passengers collect their baggage, is much better than in the circulation areas. It seems that the footage is used by the airport's maintenance department to spot damage, misuse, breakdowns, etc. It's a tetchy subject between the airport authority and the ground handling companies if there are baggage delivery delays. The handlers blame the belts, which are the responsibility of the airport to supply and maintain, and the airport blames the handlers for not using the belts according to the agreed procedures'.

As his audience was considering his response, he explained that he and Sandra had taken measurements of the shadow on the adjacent wall and had given the footage to the technical people in Garda HQ to follow up. While they were confident that this individual was highly relevant to the murder investigation, unfortunately, the most they had been able to establish at this point was an estimated height of somewhere between five foot seven inches and five foot nine.

'What about gender?' asked Detective Officer Jenny Pilger, and Wang's relief at receiving input from his audience was clear from his enthusiastic response.

'Difficult to say Jenny; they seem to be wearing a heavy weather jacket, and they're so bulky it could be male or female. About 15% of the staff in the area are female. From talking to the ground handling companies, about fifty-five staff were on duty at the time, including staff assigned to catering and boarding duties. Ground handling staff must wear Hi-Viz weather jackets when working on the airside, and they're the only category of staff we can identify in the area from other cameras at that time. However, other airport people have the authority to access that location, including the Airport Police, Gardaí, maintenance staff, fire station crews, cleaning staff, and airport terminal and duty managers.'

'Just to clarify then,' said Detective Officer Lucas Hannon, eager not to be outdone by Jenny Pilger, 'we're anxious to identify this individual because of the timing of their appearance in the hall and their suspicious behaviour, but without a clear image of their face and without knowing their weight or gender, we're hoping to use their height to compare with staff records?'

'When you put it like that, Lucas,' admitted Wang, 'it sounds like a longshot, I know, but we have to follow it up nevertheless; we're convinced it's significant'.

'I agree,' said Hennessy wanting to give Wang some support for his efforts, 'we have to follow it up. It's not as if we're exactly falling over ourselves with leads here, folks. We don't even have a murder site, for fuck's sake. Thanks, Wang and well done. Lucas, anything new from the refugee interviews?'

'Plenty actually, Gar, but nothing that progresses our murder case, I'm afraid. I'm finalising a report that should be ready in a day or so. Since they started applying for asylum, the girls are more forthcoming with information.

If we can believe them, four claim to be from Afghanistan and three from Cambodia, including the girl in the hospital. I haven't spoken directly to her, but Immigration told me, as did the girl who helped us with the apartment number in town where they were held. The Afghans say they paid US$22,000 each to be smuggled into England and spent a week travelling here. Starting with a van to some port in Libya, then a *plastic boat* as they described it, to some island in Greece, then on a truck for three days to Berlin. That's when they say they met the Cambodians. Next, all seven – they're adamant there was never an eighth girl and know nothing about our murder victim - were put in another truck for two days to some port and then on a boat. They arrived here in the middle of the night, and they were immediately transferred from the truck to a van with no windows. It only took an hour or so until they arrived at the first house, which must have been Tobin's place in Balbriggan. They thought they were in England, but one of them, the most talkative girl, figured the people handling them did not have English accents. Oh, and the Cambodians claim they paid US$20,000 each'.

'So, if they were travelling for an hour or so before they arrived in Balbriggan, we could be talking Dublin port, but you might make it from Belfast as well?' posed Jenny Pilger.

'Yep, Immigration is following that up. They reckon Rosslare and Larne would be too far. The next bit is very curious: they claim they had to leave that house in a big hurry,' said Hannon.

'So, the bastards were tipped off about our raid?' said an angry Hennessy, still reflecting on how he felt about Hannon calling him Gar.

'Seems so,' replied Hannon, 'but only six of them got back into the van, leaving the girl that assaulted our colleague behind'.

'Did they say what happened to her?' asked Hennessy.

'Nope, she was there one minute gone the next. The talkative girl got a bit nervy describing it, so maybe there was something else going on, hard to say'.

'If she was taken aside by one of the handlers, she might have been sexually assaulted?' suggested Pilger.

'That's the thing, Jenny. They maintain they were treated okay by their handlers, a few pushes and shoves along the way, and not a lot of food, but overall, they didn't have any big complaints. Of course, that could be because they're afraid they might have to testify against them or may bump into them again, I suppose?' theorised Hannon.

'Anyway,' he went on when no one made any more contributions, 'they went from there to the apartment, and we pretty much know the rest'.

'We also know that with that bollox Tobin involved, the girls were going to end up in the sex industry and the men god knows where, but not where the poor bastards thought,' said Hennessy. 'Speaking of Tobin?' he went on, looking over at Pilger.

'Right yeah, well, we're fairly sure he's still around town. A few people we've questioned said they've seen him, but none of our people, at least not yet. I'm not sure it's connected,' she continued 'but a guy that has worked for him in the past, Paul Flood, was found badly beaten up yesterday in the city centre. He was taken to hospital, but of course, he claims he fell over'.

'I've put that prick away a few times,' said Hennessy, 'and if there's a more useless, deviant, rat-faced, spineless, nasty- '

Interrupted by his phone before he could complete his description, Hennessy nodded a few times, and his mood seemed to brighten a little as he finished the call.

'Our Cambodian hospital patient wants to talk to me, according to her medics'.

'Great,' said Hannon, always trying to impress, 'will I organise a translator?'

'No need. The nurse says she speaks English'.

Chapter 46

The noise came from downstairs. It sounded like a kitchen chair moving on the wooden floor.

It was just after 4 pm but already almost dark outside.

She walked out to the top of the stairs and listened for a moment.

Nothing.

She still felt uneasy and called down. 'Is someone there?'

Nothing.

Slowly she descended, more conscious now of the darkness.

There were three doors downstairs, front, back and at the side of the townhouse, where the bins were kept in a narrow laneway.

When she had moved into the two-bedroom townhouse close to the airport, her friends told her it was too big for one person, but she liked her space. After two years, she knew the sounds in the house, and this was the first time she had ever felt nervous.

The stairs ended in the living room, and she reached out to put on the main light.

The space was empty.

She exhaled a sigh of relief.

She turned right and walked through the short hall into the kitchen, again making sure to switch on the light before she went in.

Silence.

There should be some noise: the humming from the fridge and occasionally the freezer, the water pipes rattling a little as they often did, even the ticking from the large wall clock with the knives and forks for numerals.

'Hello?' the word came out as a croak, and she had to clear her throat before she tried again. She stood in the doorway, thankful for the illumination provided by the six spotlights on the track and rail unit in the middle of the ceiling.

Two of the four chairs around the kitchen table were sideways, but she might have left them that way; housekeeping wasn't her strongest quality. Her laptop and phone were on the table where she left them. That reassured her that she wasn't being burgled.

She tried the side door, and it was unlocked, but again she had put out a bag of recyclable rubbish in the green bin earlier and could well have left the door open; she rarely locked the doors and windows before seven when she wasn't working.

The front and back doors were locked, and the only window open was the small one in the downstairs toilet, much too small for anyone to fit in.

As she stood in the middle of the kitchen, looking around one more time before she went back upstairs, the fridge began humming. Garda Sandra Whelan shook her head and tried to convince herself that she had imagined or misinterpreted the earlier noise, but she still felt uneasy.

AJ crossed the road and sat in her car. She was glad that Sandra hadn't seen her, but she was prepared with her excuse, just dropping in on her way home to give Sandra an update on the murder case. She had knocked, but nobody answered and then she found the side door open, so she went in to check that everything was in order.

In retrospect, AJ wasn't sure that Sandra would have bought it. Nevertheless, there were still too many things pointing to somebody very familiar with the airport being involved in the murder case. How did Tobin know his house was going to be raided? How come the murder site still hadn't been found? And then there was the robbery from cargo.

Sandra hadn't struck AJ as a criminal type, but then again, it was Sandra who discovered the suitcase on the CCTV, yet that hadn't progressed the investigation much. Then Sandra and Wang identified this mysterious shadow, but that didn't seem to move matters forward very much either. Sandra could have known about the raid on Tobin's house by listening to the right Garda channel.

Fortunately for AJ, both Sandra's laptop and mobile phone were left open on the kitchen table, so she was able to have a good look before she heard Sandra coming down the stairs.

Chapter 47

'I was just about to ring you boss, but I got a call that the girl in the Mater wants to talk to me; I'm on my way there now'.

'The fuck you were, Garoid. Anyhow, I have some news that may elevate your spirits. Those fuck-shits in GSOC contacted me about those larded statements of calumny relating to your recent firearm discharge in Tallaght'.

'Oh right,' said Hennessy, not fully understanding some of the words Detective Superintendent Marie Brophy was using, 'that's quick, isn't it?'

'They try to arrive at an initial position pretty quickly in case an officer needs to be taken off the streets or suspended, but in your case, I'm pleased to relate that the vainglorious pricks on your case have decided everything looks in order. Meaning you complied with protocol, meaning you won't be hung out to dry, meaning you should be able to carry a firearm again very soon, meaning you were right to protect your colleague, meaning you acted with a cornucopia of righteousness in gunning down that despicable scumbag'.

'That's excellent news, Detective Superintendent. I appreciate you letting me know, and I appreciate your support in the inquiry. Hopefully, I never have to deal with GSOC again; they have a way of making you feel like you shot Kennedy or something, very unnerving, I'd have to say' said a relieved Hennessy, gripping the steering wheel with delight and an easing of stress at the same time. He was confident that he had acted in full adherence to the rules for discharging a weapon, but at the same time, he had heard stories of GSOC finding fault where there was none, so as far as he was concerned, it could have gone either way.

'You're more than welcome, Detective. I'm just glad that it was the steaming pile of shite lying on the street with a gunshot and not one of our own. I'll let you continue with your interview. Still, I want an update this evening or tomorrow morning, Saturday or no Saturday, understood?'

'Absolutely ma'am,' confirmed Hennessy, feeling his stress levels picking up again.

Chapter 48

'Isn't technology a thing of beauty?'

'Well, we live in times of 3-D printers that can make life-taking pistols, so this isn't exactly cutting edge hi-tech,' answered Nacie to Florin Ardelean's question, gazing at the finished printing structure.

'So, explain to me how this all works. I've dabbled in it before, but I'm an amateur'.

Rodney Nacie Whitney moved to the side of his freshly assembled printing machine and gave a considered response.

He explained that when he first started counterfeiting, it was a complex and expensive business. You needed big printing presses and delicate skills to cut detailed designs by hand into metal plates. It took forever. Nowadays, a kid with a decent cell phone, a scanner and a colour inkjet printer could make funny money in about ten minutes.

'So why am I spending a small fortune on this and on your services?' enquired Florin.

'Because' Nacie emphasised, 'you can easily get ten years if you're caught, so the amateurs or 'casual counterfeiters' as they call them tend to have short careers in the industry. In the US, counterfeiting is a federal felony handled by the U.S. Secret Service; in fact, that was why the Secret Service was originally created'.

'So, which is more important then, the equipment or the person using it?' Florin probed.

With just the two men in the small warehouse beside the Curragh racecourse in County Kildare, Nacie got the impression his employer was testing his knowledge of the business, as well as his skill set.

'It has varied over the years,' he began, 'depending on which side is gaining the upper hand in this centuries-old battle between currency manufacturers and counterfeiters.'

'Did you know,' he went on, 'there is an awards ceremony for protecting the integrity of currencies? The International Association of Currency Affairs – based in

Texas, would you believe – has been recognising people and governments that come up with new ways of making notes and coins hard to copy for over a decade. They even have a Currency Hall of Fame for individuals that have excelled at it!'

'Get away!' Florin was impressed. 'And do counterfeiters have a similar scheme?'

'There's an idea,' replied a smiling Whitney.

'In my opinion,' he continued, 'there are three key steps in getting it right and staying out of jail: identifying the security features in the notes, reproducing them, and distributing the end product. Let me go through them'.

For the next fifteen minutes, Whitney regaled Florin with the facts and fables of the industry; at times in cops and robbers humorous terms; at other times as a profoundly serious business with profoundly serious consequences for those involved.

'As the $100 bill is the most commonly forged note in the world, the US Bureau of Engraving and Printing has been at the forefront of currency security. Sterling is also popular amongst counterfeiters, it's the most forged currency, and the Bank of England is constantly coming up with new ways to stop us. That's why they followed Canada and Australia with the plastic notes because they could insert holograms.'

'Right, so with all that, you have everything you need to make the perfect forgery then?' asked Ardelean.

'So far so good,' Nacie answered, 'and you have the perfect distribution plan for the finished product? Passing it off in nightclubs and vending machines is for amateurs; sooner or later, it gets professionally scanned by machines that can pick up even the most accurate counterfeit note. Then the authorities are notified, and the chase begins. In the US, you could have a Secret Service team on your tail in a matter of days. Interpol and Europol also have specialist divisions tracking down forgers, including programmes whereby manufacturers of particular printers and paper let them know about any new or suspicious purchasers. You need a better plan than that for the volume you're talking about, Florin'.

'You leave all that to me, Nacie; you'll be safe and sound back stateside with nothing to worry about'.

Chapter 49

Kate Gleeson did not like school hockey training on Saturday mornings at the River Valley Education for All School in Swords. In fact, she wasn't enthusiastic about much of anything since she started secondary school six months ago. Most of her friends from primary school had gone to a private secondary school in Dublin city centre. They got to head off on the bus every morning for great adventures while she walked for fifteen minutes through endless housing estates in a brown school uniform that she loathed.

Her mother said they couldn't afford private school fees and that the local secondary school had an excellent reputation.

Kate pointed out that her friends were wearing casual clothes, going to trendy teen cafes for lunch and shopping in all the branded shops after school every day while she was stuck with a frumpy uniform eating lunch in the school canteen and doing sports and homework clubs when classes finished. Her mother replied that she was working extra shifts as it was just to pay the bills and that

Kate should be grateful for what she had instead of always wanting more.

It wasn't fair Kate would snap back; she hated her school, and she hated her classmates, and she hated her life.

The conversation usually finished with Kate storming off to her room, adding that she hated her mother as well before slamming the door.

Her mother knew that she didn't really mean it. Teenage hormones were turning her beautiful daughter into a moody witch, but at the same time, she felt guilty that she couldn't do a better job supporting her.

When her shifts allowed, Eileen Gleeson waited for Kate outside the school's sports pitch on Saturday mornings after training to treat her to ice cream and some shopping at the local retail centre.

This Saturday morning was quite sunny for February in Ireland, so she hoped Kate would be in good form and happy to see her. She'd even take a frown as a positive sign rather than the usual angry, eye-rolling expressions and the silent treatment. This morning, she hadn't said a word at breakfast even though Eileen had got up early to make her pancakes.

After Kate's silent exit, Eileen went back to bed for a few hours to catch up on sleep as she had been working night shifts most of the week.

When she woke up, she didn't have much time to shower and get ready, and she was in too much of a rush when she left the house to notice the dark red saloon car parked about 50 metres down the road, and the occupant who got out and followed her; an occupant she might well have recognised.

The first- and second-year's hockey training was coached by Miss Sycamore. They were immediately followed by Mr. White's third and fourth-year teams. Therefore, the changing rooms and adjacent car park were high-activity zones when Eileen arrived.

Kate emerged from the changing rooms talking to another girl, who hugged her goodbye and got into a waiting car. Eileen had to restrain herself from hugging her daughter too, as that was high up on the 'most-fucking-embarrassing-mother-moment charts'.

Still, she had to beam and marvel at her daughter, bursting with pride. Kate was tall and slim with shoulder-length brunette hair and legs that seemed to go on forever.

'Hey, you! How did training go? You look great! Fancy an ice cream? Who was the pal you were talking to?'

Her daughter shrugged and fell into step with her as they made their way through more rows of houses on the ten-minute walk to the shops.

Strong rays of sunshine were breaking through the glass roofs along the malls, so it wasn't out of place that the individual following them was wearing sunglasses. Blue jeans and a black leather jacket completed the outfit.

There were throngs of people in the malls leading off the main entrance on a sunny Saturday afternoon, so it was relatively easy to stay out of their gaze. Still, sometimes there were so many customers in the trendy shops, they went missing for a few minutes.

Armed with sprinkled cones and coffees, they were women on a mission as they systematically browsed every fashion, shoes, and accessories outlet.

With long queues at all the changing rooms, they were usually twenty minutes inside, and there even seemed to be a friendly banter breaking out between them; certainly, there were smiles.

At least one purchase was made as Kate carried a bag when they emerged from one Spanish fast-fashion giant.

After several tiring hours, mother and daughter were passing through the food court when a chorus of high-pitched shrieks erupted from one of the tables. Kate's face lit up when she saw a group of girls calling her. Words were quickly exchanged, and Eileen took out her purse, gave Kate a note, and watched her skip off excitedly to join her noisy friends. Eileen seemed happy her daughter was with this group of girls.

Eileen walked out of the shopping centre and headed up through Swords main street. It looked like the surveillance was an uneventful waste of time.

Until Eileen walked into the outside-heated beer garden of Taylor's Hotel and Bar, leaned over to warmly embrace and kiss a customer seated at a table for two, and take her seat opposite.

Well, knock me over with a fucking feather, thought AJ as she continued past and walked briskly back to her car, trying to take in what she had just witnessed. She could think about it on her way home. She needed to get ready before her big night out in the city centre.

Missing something normal

spotting something strange

needing to stay formal

soon there will be change

Chapter 50

Miriam Hennessy half knocked and stuck her head into the study at the same time.

'Want to go for a walk by the harbour, Gar? It's a lovely afternoon?'

He had been subdued all day, and she knew he was having a hard time with this murder case. Working long hours every day of the week was nothing new when he was assigned to a big case, but this was definitely the highest-profile one he had headed up. Their daughter Anais was staying with a friend in Bray, so there was just the two of them in the house.

After breakfast, he had gone into the study, and she heard him making several phone calls, including one that must have been to his boss as he used the term 'ma'am'. It wasn't just the murder investigation that was bugging him, she figured; it was AJ Jenkinson's involvement as well. Miriam knew they had a falling out in Limerick, but he never talked about the details, so she never pushed it.

They met when she had just qualified as a nurse and was working in her first job at Naas General Hospital in Kildare, near where she grew up. One night, he arrived at the hospital helping a colleague who had been beaten up while trying to make an arrest. When she brought his colleague's bloodied tunic out of the treatment room, Garoid was waiting outside, and they got chatting. He was like a big huggable bear, she thought. A few months later, they got engaged, and when Garoid was promoted and transferred to Dublin, they bought an old fisherman's cottage in the north Dublin town of Skerries.

'Sure thing Mir, give me a few minutes'.

He had all his case files laid out on the desk in front of him, and he was re-reading everything from the start to see what they had missed. That's what he was taught in Templemore College, and that's what more senior, experienced colleagues had told him time and again.

Go back to the start. Work the case from the evidence and the interviews. What did we miss? What do we have that we don't know we have? There are no shortcuts; it's hard graft that will deliver results. That brought him right back to the phone call received by the duty cleaning supervisor last Sunday evening and the response of the cleaning staff member who found the suitcase. Time to have a much closer look at those two, thought Hennessy.

His interview with the injured refugee had been a waste of time. She was playing him to try to strengthen her asylum case. He felt sorry for her for what she had gone through, but he was fucking annoyed that she had absolutely nothing to contribute to his case, and he wasn't sanctioning an officer on her door any longer; that was a matter for Immigration now.

She was adamant that there was never another girl in their group; there was just the seven of them. Nor did she have a reason she was singled out in the house in Balbriggan and left behind. She was terrified that she would be assaulted or worse, but there seemed to be almost no time between her handlers going and the doors being kicked in. She claimed she didn't know that they were the police and was defending herself when she attacked the female officer. She continuously apologised for hurting her and wanted to meet her to apologise in person, she had told a disbelieving Hennessy.

When he asked her why she hadn't helped him the first time they met, she said she was still terrified that the people handling them would find out and find her.

Hennessy had spent a lot of time planning what he would say to Marie Brophy and how he would say it. If she thought he was making no progress almost a week on, that was one thing, but if he gave the impression that his big emphasis on Tobin was not panning out and he didn't know the next steps to progress the case, that was something a lot worse.

If he was taken off the case by Brophy or if she assigned another detective to work with him, they both came down to the one thing: he had failed, and his career might as well be over.

In the end, he decided not to fudge it. He reported what his team was doing and why they were proceeding in the way they were, and what direction they were moving in. He told her about the interviews they had conducted and the technical work behind the scenes to identify the murder victim and establish where she was killed. Finally, he came clean and admitted he had contacted a few senior detectives he knew and bounced some ideas off them.

He tried to sound upbeat and confident, but he didn't want to seem over-confident because there was nothing in his update to justify such an attitude.

When he finished with his 'roll the sleeves up and go back over everything from the start spiel', he was sure that she was going to fuck him out of it and call him much worse names that he didn't understand.

She had used some curse words all right. She had used words he wasn't awfully familiar with, something about not wanting to use asperity in replying to him and that the investigation seemed aqueous in strength at the moment was how he heard them. Still, she didn't blast him out of it, and he was grateful for that.

Maybe it was because it was Saturday morning, he thought. He knew she played golf in St Margaret's golf course on Saturdays, or perhaps she had already planned to replace him first thing Monday morning. Still, she seemed quite supportive and reassuring, telling him at the end of the call that cases like this often benefitted from the accretion he had outlined. He definitely heard her use *accretion,* and he was fairly sure that meant a gradual building up of something; at least, he hoped she intended it that way. He found Brophy hard to figure out. She was known to keep her private life private, but he had heard there was a messy divorce in her background, something not unheard of in their job. Whatever way it goes, he was feeling better for ringing her.

His walk along Skerries Harbour arm in arm with Miriam, followed by two cups of coffee from the mobile kiosk, was a welcome relief from his job. They talked about the weather, and they talked about their beautiful Anais, and they talked about where they might go for their summer holidays.

They talked about everything but his job, and he knew that was the way Miriam planned it.

Chapter 51

The music was still in background mode when AJ entered The Brazen Judge just after 7 pm, but she had frequented this pub enough times to realise that it would get a lot louder as the night wore on. Her hair was down, and she was dressed in a short black skirt with black tights and black suede pumps.

Their usual corner was already occupied by what looked like a hen party, so she continued on towards the dance area at the back before seeing three faces that she recognised. Dominick was deep in conversation when he saw her and jumped up to welcome her.

'Hi Dom, good to see you,' she said as she hugged him, turning to see the lovely smiley face of Shauna Patton getting up behind him.

'Shauna! You look great!' she uttered as they embraced.

'You too, AJ, how are you?'

Before she could answer, Louise Brennan was wrapping her arms around her.

'AJ, you beautiful thing!' oozed Louise, not letting go too quickly.

Dominick untangled them, 'okay, everyone, sit down. It's still my round. AJ, what are you having gorgeous?'

'White wine, please, Dom'.

Within minutes, three more of the gang had arrived, Martha Tazzerman, Mike Thompson and Ray Fulton, and the buzz and merriment were just the same as the old days. Everyone fell into their most comfortable and fun-loving version of themselves as old stories were dredged up, re-told in embellished terms, and laughed at uproariously as if being heard for the first time.

Drinks were flowing, the music as expected was getting louder, and soon the whole crew were up on the dance floor giving it everything.

When a slow set came on, AJ found herself up close and personal with Ray Fulton. Her face leaned into the crook of his neck, his hands slowly circling her waist and lower back.

By the time the second slow song came on, Eric Clapton's *Wonderful Tonight*, they were kissing passionately, and AJ was relaxing into his muscular frame.

'You smell like....man,' she whispered, feeling stupid immediately for such a cringey comment.

'Thanks, AJ, you really know how to sweet-talk a guy!' he mocked in response. She didn't continue the conversation out of sheer embarrassment but snuggled up even closer.

She had known Ray for years and had always thought him good fun, but tonight she found him particularly attractive, thoughts that were fuelled no doubt from copious glasses of white wine.

When he gently pulled away and took her hand to lead her over to their table to collect their things and then out to the line of waiting taxis, she was happy to comply. Jeers and whistles from their carousing pals as the amorous couple left the heaving pub were heard but not acknowledged.

Work is only worth it

if you get the balance right.

It's play that gives the rush

and this could be the night!

Chapter 52

Twenty kilometres west of The Brazen Judge, Detective Jenny Pilger was driving under the arched entrance to Tallaght University Hospital. Beside her was Garda Helen Nolan, who had earlier reported the possible sighting in a fast-food cafe near the Guinness brewery of a suspect who was wanted for questioning by the airport murder team. She reported her finding and position to Control and was instructed to keep the suspect under surveillance until further notice.

Thirty minutes later, Jenny Pilger picked her up down the road from the cafe and told her they needed a positive identification before they moved in to arrest the suspect. Control had tried to contact the Detective Inspector in charge of the murder inquiry, but when his phone was constantly engaged, the next person on the call-out list was Jenny Pilger.

The window of the cafe was steamed up from the volume of customers and lack of ventilation. Jenny was not going to risk going in herself or sending an undercover officer to make a positive identification, given the violent nature of the suspect and the inhospitable welcome the area had for Gardaí, undercover or otherwise.

A light rain had started to fall, and everyone who left the cafe either had a hat, an umbrella or a hoodie, so getting a clear view was proving very difficult. Jenny was conscious that an Emergency Response Unit was on standby in the area and a marked car and a motorcycle, but she was also quite confident that if this was the individual they thought it was, he would be armed.

After a tense hour of watching the front door and hoping they weren't spotted, a stooped figure in a black hoodie and dark jeans exited the cafe and trotted briskly to a parked car nearby. Jenny Pilger and Helen Nolan looked at each other and nodded.

'If that's not him,' said Jenny, 'it's his doppelganger!'

Having reported the situation to Control, Pilger decided to follow the suspect until he stopped the car rather than risk a shootout by forcing his vehicle to stop.

Fifteen minutes later, she followed his car into the hospital while speed dialling a number on her mobile phone.

Thankfully, this time it was answered.

'Gar, it's Jenny, we're pulling up at the hospital where Ger Cosgrave is still a patient, and we're fairly sure that the guy we're following is Alfie Tobin'.

Chapter 53

The Sunday noon shift sounded like a good idea when she agreed to it, but AJ deeply regretted it now. She should have put in for a day off instead of a later start.

Ray was so good about it earlier but she still felt awkward and embarrassed. He wanted to get her a taxi but she insisted on walking to clear her head, she said. When she got a few streets away, she rang a taxi and just got home in time to shower, take headache tablets, and get another taxi to work.

Sandra Whelan had said something to her about an intruder as their shifts crossed, but AJ was trying so hard not to breathe on her and not to throw up that she passed it off without comment.

Now she was sitting at her computer, popping mints continuously and listening to Mossy Owens have an argument with a highly agitated woman at the public counter who said her car was clamped outside the departures floor while she was wheeling her invalided sister into the terminal. She was incensed that her vehicle could be clamped in such circumstances when she only left it for a few minutes, and she wanted Mossy to do something about it,

'I'm sorry, Madam, but the Airport Police is a separate agency to An Garda Siochana, and they are responsible for clamping. I'm sure if you made your case to – '.

'I've already done that!' she interrupted, 'but they wouldn't do anything about it, and I refuse to pay the fine'.

Over and back, over and back, the argument went on. AJ desperately needed to get fresh air for her throbbing head, but she was afraid that if she went too close to the public counter, both Mossy and the complaining lady would see and smell how bad a state she was in.

After another ten minutes, there was still no sign of the woman backing down. She was now demanding to see Mossy's superior, which he did not appreciate, pointing out that clamping signs were clearly displayed. It would have been straightforward and just as quick to use the multi-storey car park. He explained that the airlines offered a service for departing wheelchair passengers whereby they were met on the departures road, wheeled through the various stages and on to the aircraft.

She knew all that she countered loudly, but her sister had to travel at short notice for medical reasons. The car was only left unattended for a matter of minutes, she proclaimed.

AJ and Mossy and every other Garda at the airport station had heard it .many times before. The answer was always the same: please take it up with the Airport Police.

As this particular lady seemed to be in it for the long-haul and Mossy seemed to be getting more annoyed, AJ decided it was now or never and got up from her desk, picked up her cap and made her exit with her face as hidden as possible by pretending to adjust her cap so that her hair wasn't sticking out.

When she got outside, AJ was so relieved she kept walking and breathing deeply without realising that she'd forgotten to bring a radio set with her. Foot patrols were supposed to be only taken with a radio set in case an emergency arose.

As if emergencies were regular occurrences at this station, AJ thought when she discovered her omission. Then she remembered that she had her mobile phone in her pocket. She had turned it off in case Ray rang, so she quickly switched it on and let the station know that she would return shortly to pick up a radio set but, in the meanwhile, would use her mobile if anything arose. She smiled as it struck her that Mossy hadn't answered, so the argument with the clamping lady must have continued.

She walked around the car parks for nearly an hour, not so much to battle crime as to allow her headache to ease. Once her head didn't thump so much, AJ decided she was well enough to continue investigating the hunch she had started working on a few days earlier. She was on foot this time, though, so she reckoned a little help would be needed.

When she rang the Airport Police Control Room, she explained her query, but the person who answered didn't seem knowledgeable in the area or maybe wasn't keen on helping her. Her colleagues in the station often commented on friction between the Airport Police and the Gardaí, but AJ hadn't met with any outright hostility; maybe a slight unease at times, but that was to be expected given their somewhat overlapping roles yet quite different training, operational and legislative frameworks.

Next, she rang the Duty Office, where the Airport Duty Manager is based but was told that she was attending to something at the Information Desk. AJ didn't want to leave a message, so she told the person who answered that she would try again later.

There were a few people she didn't want to ask, but as she was scrolling down through her contact list to see who to try next, she noticed one of the passenger baggage trolley staff getting into their trolley-towing jeep. She walked over to the passenger side of the vehicle and beckoned to the driver to lower the window on the passenger door. As he did so, she couldn't help but smile at the irony of her standing as far away as possible from the driver so he couldn't smell alcohol off her breath. How many drivers had she stopped over the years and asked them to lower their windows precisely so she could try to detect the smell of alcohol?

'Hi, I'm AJ from the station here. Can I ask you something, please?'

The driver looked about fourteen. AJ knew a lot of the trolley staff were sons and daughters of airport employees and worked part-time or during the summer to save money for college or a backpacking holiday or, in some cases, emigration. She noticed he was looking at her uniform and seemed a little hesitant.

'Eh, sure, did I do something wrong?'

'No, not at all,' she reassured him. 'I'm trying to find out if there are particular locations around the airport where unused trolleys are stored? I don't mean the ones you collect. I mean the big, covered ones for loading and unloading planes?'

'There are marked off areas for parking them around the piers,' he answered, relieved at the query.

'Yeah, I know about them, and I know where they do the welding repairs on them over beside the Fire Station. I'm wondering if you've seen collections of them anywhere else on your travels?'

'Sometimes you see a few of them in the hangars,' he replied after thinking about it for a little bit, 'I think the mechanics might use them for carrying engine parts and stuff'.

'I've checked there as well. Maybe somewhere more secluded or off the beaten track; you have to check all kinds of nooks and crannies around the place looking for passenger trolleys, don't you?'

The young driver thought about it for another while but was nodding his head as he did so.

'Sorry, can't think of anywhere else'.

'Not to worry, thanks anyway,' said AJ taking out her mobile again to look at her contacts as the jeep pulled off with about twenty trolleys in tow.

The last of the trolleys was passing when the jeep stopped a little abruptly, and the driver leaned out the door.

'There's a bunch of old wrecked ones dumped over behind the Snow and Ice equipment building, but I don't think they use them anymore,' he shouted and then continued on his way.

AJ put her thumb up to say thanks and put her phone away as she walked briskly back to the station. I should be fine to drive the patrol car now, she thought.

Chapter 54

All the participants in the room had been named, and the time, date and location noted on tape when Detective Inspector Hennessy surveyed the two men sitting across the table from him.

First, he gazed distastefully at the solicitor and then at his client, who had a plaster over his right eye.

'Can we start with last Sunday; you arrived at Dublin Airport on a flight from Berlin, yes? Can you tell me the purpose of your trip, please?'

Silence.

Hennessy looked down at the folder in front of him and deliberately let time go by.

Eventually, the solicitor broke the silence.

'My client has a right to leave the country whenever he wants to Detective. It's not a crime'.

'Detective Inspector,' Hennessy corrected him.

The solicitor narrowed his eyes at Hennessy.

'I was making a porno film if you must fucking know. I'm in big demand,' said Alfie Tobin in as sleazy a tone as he could, deliberately staring at Detective Jenny Pilger.

Pilger didn't flinch but thought back to when she'd arrested him and wished she had hit him harder.

'You could have blinded me, you ugly bitch!' he snarled.

Pilger didn't react outwardly, but her eyes sparkled.

'The body of a young girl was found at Dublin Airport around the same time, and I believe your client may know something about that crime,' said Hennessy getting back on topic and deliberately putting the question to the solicitor, taking the focus off Tobin to make him look secondary to the proceedings.

'I don't know anything about any fucking murder,' Tobin spat back at the Detective Inspector.

'So it was just a coincidence that you were passing through at that time?' queried Jenny Pilger.

'Fuck off, you fucking slut!'

'Can you please inform your client that there's no need for that kind of language?' said Hennessy to the solicitor.

The solicitor didn't respond, just stared impassively.

Hennessy let time pass again as he shuffled some of the gruesome photos of the murder victim so his guests could see them.

'Within hours of this body being found, a raid took place on a property, registered in your name, in Balbriggan. An asylum seeker was found there, along with evidence of six others; can you explain that please?' queried Hennessy trying to move things on.

'No, nothing to do with me, some bastard must've broken in'.

'Are you aware of a break-in? Did you report it to the Gardaí?'

Tobin replied with a chuckle.

'Human trafficking is a serious offence,' said Hennessy looking directly at Tobin now.

'Nothing to do with me,' he answered.

'So these six asylum seekers that you say you know nothing about. They were transferred from your house to a city centre apartment, just behind the Four Courts. Can you tell me what you know about that?' said Hennessy pushing on more quickly now.

'Fuck all,' said Tobin.

'So, how do you explain your fingerprints being found there?' Hennessy shot back.

Pilger wanted to scream *yessss,* but she showed no reaction.

Tobin didn't respond. His solicitor kept his eyes down.

Hennessy let several minutes pass.

'They were moved from the apartment, where, as I say, we found your fingerprints, to a house in Oldbawn, Tallaght. Do you know anything about that?'

Nothing from Tobin.

'The driver was a colleague of yours, Ger Cosgrave, who was subsequently arrested leaving that property. Can you tell me anything about that?'

Tobin stared at the wall over Hennessy's head.

Hennessy turned to Pilger to take up the running.

'You were arrested last night outside the hospital where Cosgrave is being treated; can you tell us what you were doing there?' asked Pilger.

'Visiting, slut!' barked Tobin aggressively. He rubbed the side of his head as if to erase pain.

'In the middle of the night?' she probed.

No response from Tobin.

'Carrying a firearm?' she continued swiftly.

'You have no evidence that my client was visiting Mr Cosgrave or intended him any harm. On the contrary, the firearm was for personal protection; it's a perilous city out there,' said the solicitor.

Pilger and Hennessy let more time pass, shuffling papers to make it look like they had more cards to play than they were showing.

'Okay, the position is that we're drawing up charges for human trafficking, possession of a firearm and resisting arrest. We're still investigating several other matters, including forensics on the firearm, to establish if it was used in any other crimes and may bring further charges at a future date. Do you have anything to say?' This time, Hennessy gazed straight into Tobin's eyes.

Tobin's solicitor nudged him to say nothing, then looked at Hennessy.

'My client has no comment to make at this time'.

As Hennessy was officially closing the interview and turning off the tape recorder, his phone, face down on the desk and on vibrate, gave a shuddering motion. When he checked who was calling, he briskly swiped the reject icon.

Pilger opened the door and asked the Garda stationed outside to take Tobin back to his cell.

Sometimes after interviews like these, comments are made between solicitor and client or to the interviewers when the tape recorder has been switched off, so Hennessy was in the habit of taking his time tidying up his paperwork. There had even been the odd occasion where an off-the-cuff utterance proved useful in the subsequent prosecution.

He also wanted to congratulate Pilger on the arrest and ask her to take a closer look at the two cleaning staff members involved in discovering the body.

Now, however, his eyes were drawn to the incoming text from AJ.

I've found your murder scene.

Chapter 55

It must be what the inside of a small abattoir looks like after a busy day, thought Calvin Walshe as he peered in. The canvas covers of the baggage dolly were firmly tied down on all sides, and the dried blood, even under the strong arc lights that had been set up by his team, made even the strongest stomach heave. The sheer volume of blood was startling, and small collections of what seemed like human tissue were scattered around the floor along with cuttings of blood-spattered plastic material. Two metal objects, each about a metre long and covered in blood, were tossed in a corner.

Walshe was explaining to Detective Inspector Hennessy and Detective Jenny Pilger the approach they were taking.

The two detectives had travelled to the scene together. Hennessy congratulated Pilger on the arrest and got all the details, including the smack on the head she gave him with the butt of her gun when he refused to take his right hand from his hoodie pocket. Tobin had a firearm, phone and a few bank cards in his pocket, all now with the Lab for examination, she had informed him.

Crime scene tape had been placed around the site, which was about fifteen metres square, by the first Gardaí on the scene. Walshe had counted a total of seventeen baggage units of various sizes and states of disrepair on the site, which seemed to be a dumping ground for unusable equipment, he told them.

The site was located only 1500 metres from the passenger terminals and was accessed either by a slip road off a taxiway for the main runway or from the snow and ice equipment building directly.

The overgrown vegetation on the site and the Duty Airport Manager's comments indicated that it was considered a remote and little-used area.

Five technical staff were on site. Three concentrated on the illuminated dolly, and two checked bins and skips in the area. Photography, DNA, and fingerprints were the primary focus, with all other items of interest collected and catalogued. Measurements were also taken of the units where evidence was found and the distances between them.

As Walshe explained this to the two detectives, one of the Airport Police Inspectors, Tony Fallon, approached and introduced himself. The investigators were particularly interested in CCTV coverage of the area, but API Fallon did not have good news. There were several cameras inside and outside the snow and ice building, he explained, but none covered this area. In addition, cameras on the perimeter fence bordering the other side of the site pointed outwards, and none rotated. This dumping ground for unserviceable ground handling equipment, he pointed out, simply wasn't that important in terms of securing the airfield.

Carmel Lockton, the airport's Head of Services, also spoke to the two detectives. She had been accompanying several British police officers on a tour of the airport in preparation for the upcoming visit of the Royal couple and heard the news on her radio set.

She explained to Hennessy and Pilger that the land was zoned for an extension to the snow and ice equipment building and was only used temporarily as a transit point, from which the vehicles were collected and transported to a scrap yard. The collections were arranged by the ground handling companies in conjunction with the airport authority and took place a few times a year, depending on volume.

'When I started here 10 years ago, we only needed this building for 4 months a year and clearing snow and ice was rarely an issue. Now, the airport has grown so large we need about 100 vehicles to clear the runways, plus, the weather has worsened, so this place needs to be extended'.

'So, February would be a busy month around here, with plenty of vehicles coming and going?' asked Pilger.

'Absolutely', confirmed Lockton.

AJ stood within earshot of the conversations, watching the activity going on within and around the crime scene tape. Although it hadn't been officially confirmed that the suitcase victim had been murdered in the baggage dolly, there was no doubt in AJ's mind.

Her thoughts were on the terror the poor girl must have gone through in that dirty, dark, cramped space in her final moments. She was also thinking how dismissive Garoid Hennessy had been of her when he arrived on the scene.

She'd tried to explain her reasoning for suspecting an airside murder site, but he brushed past her. She had followed him to tell him about Sandra Whelan's findings relating to the first reported smell but he kept moving towards the dolly, so AJ backed off.

When she saw Detective Sergeant Wang get out of a Garda patrol car behind the entourage of technical and emergency vehicles, she approached him. Explicitly, she asked him to bring the matter of the reported smell to Hennessey's attention as she considered it significant. Wang was preoccupied with this key development in the case but he was much more polite and respectful. He made a point of thanking her for her help, and then he too, continued on.

Chapter 56

Late on Sunday afternoon, The Ark public house was beginning to empty of the family lunch clientele, leaving only the soccer fans watching an English premiership game. A few hardy souls were braving the cold February weather to enjoy a cigarette in the outside smoking area. The usual sprinkling of airport uniforms was on show.

AJ found a quiet spot near the window and ordered an Irish whiskey and water from the lounge girl, who approached her as soon as she was seated. She wanted to take her coat off but was wearing her uniform underneath, so she thought better of it. Alcohol might not be appropriate, considering the bellyful she had consumed the night before, she thought, but the shock of opening up the canvas on that baggage dolly a few hours ago, combined with the frustration of trying to deal with her former work partner, and the tiredness that was building from her late night convinced her that a stiff drink was required.

It had taken her no time to find the location for old equipment that the young lad from the trolley section had told her about. As she started poking around the different units, she had felt an increasing sense of dread.

She grew more nervous with each covered or closed dolly as she untangled, unzipped, and unbolted the openings. She was almost hoping that she was wrong, that she was way off, that she had embarked on a wild goose chase, but the more she had toured and studied the baggage handling halls, the more confident she became that the murder took place somewhere on the airside of the airport.

She had searched all the offices, storerooms, and equipment rooms in the locality without finding anything. It was only when focusing on the footage of the suitcase spotted by Sandra on the baggage dolly that it had struck her that those same dollies could be closed up and were big enough to kill and dismember. If that was the case, it was now much easier for the killer or killers to move not just the body and its parts but the entire murder scene.

It became a mobile murder site; a horror show on wheels.

When her whiskey arrived, AJ paid for it, poured a small drop of water, and took a large gulp. She shivered at once from the hit, and it reminded her why she never drank whiskey on a night out. It was far too potent.

Of course, there was other airport equipment that could fit the same purpose, such as the catering trolleys or the igloos and unit load devices used for transporting cargo or even some of the vehicles used for carrying large aircraft parts, but only the baggage dolly would be considered regular and routine in the baggage sorting area. Any other vehicle might arouse suspicion.

Nevertheless, as she conducted her searches on the apron and in the hangars and the cargo and fire station areas, she made a point of checking everything on wheels, with a cover that could conceal a body.

There were only 3 dollies left to uncover. As she began opening the first one, AJ began to feel nauseous. There seemed to be some kind of organic droppings emerging from under the flaps of the canvas covers, and she became increasingly aware of a foul smell. She flung back a loose cover with her right hand while using the left to hold over her nose and mouth. Some of the old, rusted catering trays inside had plastic food cartons left on them. Their contents had been visited and revisited by many different scavengers as far as AJ could see, some of whom were still present.

Moving swiftly on to the vehicle behind it, the yellow-coloured sides were well tied down, and the wheels and tow bar appeared quite workable compared to its neighbours. From the outside, there were no signs of anything untoward about it. The zip holding down the front cover opened very quickly, in fact too quickly, as AJ wasn't ready for the repulsive spectacle in front of her. She had to step back and gasp before slowly peeking in again, opening the flap wider this time to allow in more light. Although nobody could be prepared for the unexpected stench of days-old blood, her nostrils didn't seem to react as much as her eyes did. When she had satisfied herself that this was it, she reached into her pocket and took out her mobile phone.

'You look like you've seen a ghost, AJ?'

Startled out of her recollections, AJ looked up to see Larry Smalling, one of the managers, smiling down at her.

'Sorry Larry, I was miles away. How are you?'

'Great, thanks, and you? I didn't know you were a whiskey drinker?' he said, looking down at her branded glass.

'I'm not! Just having a bad day, but I'm fine, really. While I have you, Larry, can I ask you something?'

'Sure, AJ, fire away'.

'I was in here last Monday morning, and Mossy and his pals were sitting over in the corner under the TV, do you remember?'

'Eh, yeah, you were in very early, asking about the girl found murdered in the suitcase?'

'That's right. You didn't happen to know any of the guys that Mossy was with, did you? I think they're on some sports committee. The only reason I'm asking is I thought I recognised one of them, but I can't recall his name?'

'The hurling club committee, yep, I know them'.

As soon as Larry told her the names, AJ thanked him and left, leaving her unfinished whiskey on the table.

Boys will be boys

playing with men's toys

plotting in the pub

about the hurling club

was it just for show?

who'd they want to know?

need to pick a side

nowhere left to hide

Chapter 57

Monday mornings in the airport Garda station were like every other morning. Sergeant Tim Coady was thinking on his way in, quiet.

However, he was told by the officer staffing the front desk that a Royal visit meeting had already started in the conference room, someone from HQ had rung on behalf of DI Hennessy to book the room for a 10 am meeting about the murder case, and the Garda National Economic Crime Bureau had called to say they were carrying out an operation in the passenger terminal this morning.

'Is that it,' asked Coady mischievously to Garda Leah Regan, 'so all's quiet in other words?'

The first two pieces of information didn't surprise Coady with the Royal visit coming up. He had heard about the finding of the murder site the previous day. However, the third piece of information was slightly unusual as GNECB didn't have to inform the local station when they were on site. Still, he appreciated the courtesy.

He had experience of specialist units carrying out undercover surveillance and making high profile arrests at the airport without notifying the station. That had led to a few uncomfortable and embarrassing situations, including a stand-off between one of his officers and a guy from the Criminal Assets Bureau who was believed to be acting suspiciously and refusing to identify himself.

He was still checking emails when AJ arrived in. Knowing she had been on duty at the time, he asked her if she had gone over to the location. AJ seemed pretty unsettled talking about it. It was only after a few minutes of conversation that it dawned on Coady.

'Christ AJ, *you* found the dolly!'

AJ didn't respond. She just looked down at her keyboard.

Coady realised he had said that a little too loud, so he lowered his voice this time as he pulled over a seat beside her.

'I'm sorry, I didn't know that. All I heard was that the dolly had been found, and a major technical operation had commenced. Well done you! That must have been some shock? You know you can take some time off after an event like that, and you know you can reach out to the counselling service? How did you figure that out? Was it all the stuff you were doing on the left luggage the other day? Jesus, it's a bit of a jump from looking up lost bag policies to finding the dolly where a girl was butchered a mile the other side of the airport!'

As he was speaking, he realised that he was getting far too excited about it and asking far too many questions. He had never found a dead body or the site of a bloody murder, so he couldn't really relate to how AJ must be feeling. He knew enough to know that he needed to back off and give her space, though. And to support her. He was just about to say something along those lines when AJ looked up.

'If it's okay with you, Tim, I have to write up my report on finding it, so I'd like to get on with it?'

'Of course, of course,' he answered, putting the seat back where he got it and going back to his emails. He hadn't even mentioned the other things going on this morning, he thought as he walked away.

The five people using the conference room had only just left when Hennessy's team began arriving. Wang came in chatting to Mossy Owens but still made a point of saying hello to everyone in the station Coady noted. Pilger and Hannon were also reasonably friendly, he thought, but when Hennessy appeared, he didn't make much of an effort to greet anyone. It wasn't that he was rude about it, Coady decided, just that he was a little too full of himself as if they were lucky to have him in their presence. Then again, Hennessy must be under a lot of pressure with this case. The discovery of the luggage dolly was splashed all over the headlines, and journalists were congregating over by the boundary fence beside the site. The black sheeting put up by the technical people and the white tent erected over the dolly itself ensured they couldn't see anything of interest. When Hennessy closed the door of the conference room, Coady changed his mind about the DI. He never even nodded to AJ, he thought, and she was the one that made the discovery. The miserable bastard, he cursed.

'Okay', said Hennessy kicking off the briefing, 'Walshe and his people have been working during the night. I'll contact him as soon as we're done here. Lucas, I want you to follow up on that equipment dump. Who actually owns that baggage cart? Do the companies share them? Can anyone drive them? Who decides when a piece of equipment is moved over there, and are any records kept? Surely, all of this stuff is insured, so they must keep records? And double-check all the bins in the area; there must be blood-soaked clothes dumped somewhere. Find out the bin collection schedule'.

'Wang, you've done good work on the camera footage, so I want you to examine every single piece of recording from the last week involving vehicles and people moving around that part of the airport. We must be able to pick up something'.

'Jenny, I've asked you to start looking in more detail at the two cleaning staff involved at the very beginning. The one who got the call and the one who responded. We've already spoken to both of them, so dig those interviews out and start delving more into their backgrounds. You know the stuff: bank accounts, lifestyles, previous jobs, etc. If you need a court order for anything, just let me know. But don't approach them directly. We don't want to spook them if they were involved. We've already checked criminal records for all the employees we've interviewed. Nothing much came up but focus on those two and check for name changes, family records, blah, blah, blah. And before I forget, well done, Jenny on that Tobin arrest, good stuff. Any questions, anyone have anything to add?'

The three team members had been nodding eagerly and taking notes as their boss was speaking. This breakthrough was a coup for all of them.

Jenny and Wang shared a look. They had congratulated AJ on their way into the meeting, and now they wondered why Hennessy hadn't mentioned her. She was the one who made the breakthrough. They hadn't been within a hundred miles of figuring out where the body might be, and AJ wasn't even on the team.

The meeting continued for another half hour, with each of the participants asking questions and teasing out scenarios and lines of thought. There was much more energy in the group, a feeling that they were getting close to a result.

Wang asked if he could continue to involve Sandra Whelan as her help was invaluable, and Hannon requested two of the detectives working the case in headquarters to be assigned to help him with the equipment site work. Hannon also told his boss that he was planning to visit the site as soon as the briefing was over. Hennessy took his point; he was the only one not present the previous day and was anxious to get stuck in.

As they continued the conversation, Hennessy's phone rang. He snatched it up when he saw Calvin Walshe's name appear. It was a short call, with Hennessy nodding his way through it and thanking Walshe before he hung up.

'Not that it's a big surprise,' he said, 'but Walshe confirms that the blood is from our victim. He says the two metal objects found are aircraft maintenance tools: a torque wrench and safety wire pliers'.

Chapter 58

He had been in bigger interview rooms, but he had also been in more putrid ones, he was thinking. When he was approached by a male and female after he had cleared the security screening process, he wasn't particularly surprised; it was an occupational hazard. Better it happened on the way out than on the way in, he figured.

However, the two officers did strike him as particularly young, much more so than he had encountered in other jurisdictions.

They had left him alone now for about twenty minutes, but he wasn't too concerned. He had nothing incriminating in his luggage, which he was quite sure they were now checking, and he had plenty of time before his US flight departed.

There were muffled sounds from the public announcement system, and a few minutes ago, he heard the loud drone of what sounded like a large aircraft being pushed back from its parking stand.

When the two officers returned, they put the bag he had allowed them to check on the floor beside him. They knew that he knew they had found nothing incriminating. His checked-in baggage was being searched by a colleague in the baggage hall.

They introduced themselves formally again and thanked him for his cooperation in agreeing to answer some questions. Both were assigned to the Payment Card and Counterfeit Currency Unit of the Garda National Economic Crime Bureau, based in Harcourt Square in Dublin city centre.

Garda Lorraine O'Keefe sat down first, followed by her colleague Garda Eamonn Kavanagh. They had been alerted to Rodney Whitney's trip by the US Secret Service, but his flight had arrived several hours before the information got into the hands of the right people. Such alerts from the US authorities were not uncommon, and they usually took the form of a courtesy information notice rather than any type of alert or emergency. The latter would tend to come via Interpol or Europol and were unusual and actioned urgently.

'So, Mr Whitney, you were telling us that the nature of your trip was pleasure?' asked Garda O'Keefe.

'That's correct officer, I had never been to your beautiful country before, and I wanted to spend a few days of rest and relaxation,' he replied calmly.

'Could you tell us your itinerary then, please, since you arrived?' probed O'Keefe.

'Well, I didn't have anything booked. I just travelled around without any particular plan'.

'So what kind of places did you see Mr Whitney?' she continued.

'Oh, you know, the touristy places. Unfortunately, I wasn't keeping track, and it was only a short trip. I intend to come back though and spend much longer here; they tell me Galway is worth seeing'.

'Maybe you have the receipts from your accommodation?' queried Garda Kavanagh.

'I don't request receipts officer, save the environment'.

'How did you travel, car hire?' Kavanagh went on.

'Taxis and buses; I'm not big into driving'.

The two officers had dealt with many calm and collected interviewees but Whitney gave new meaning to calm and collected, they were both thinking.

'What about your phone Mr Whitney; perhaps we could have a look at that to see where your travels took you?' ventured Kavanagh.

Whitney sat up in his seat.

'I've cooperated with your questions, officers. I've allowed you to check my cabin bag, and I'm sure you've gone through my hold bag also at this point – even though you did not have my permission and did not show me a warrant – but I have done nothing wrong, and I have a plane to catch. I am indeed carrying a cell phone and also a USB memory stick, both of which are heavily encrypted, but you will need a warrant if you want to look at them.'

'You seem very familiar with your rights Mr Whitney,' said Kavanagh, as a statement rather than a question.

'Not my first rodeo officer,' he shot back, 'now if we're done here, may I leave?'

'Certainly, Mr Whitney; thank you again for your cooperation, and we wish you a pleasant flight,' answered O'Keefe as she and her colleague stood up.

Whitney picked up his bag and walked over to the door without saying anything. He was halfway out when O'Keefe made one last effort.

'One final question Mr Whitney please: your travel documents say you had an extra bag when you arrived on Thursday morning. I hope it wasn't stolen?'

'Very observant of you, officer' Whitney smiled, 'got damaged getting off a bus. One of the wheels came off. So I left it for disposal in my hotel room.'

'In the hotel you don't remember the name of?' asked O'Keefe.

'That's it, officer,' he responded as he closed the door behind him.

The two officers met their colleague, Garda Alan Courtney, on the way back to their car. Kavanagh was ringing the airport station to let them know they were done.

'So, Courts, nothing of interest?' asked O'Keefe.

'No fucking stash of fake $100 bills if that's what you're asking, Lorraine,' replied Courtney in his broad Dublin accent.

'Didn't think so. Or no receipts, directions, phone numbers?'

'Nope, waste of time,' he replied.

Kavanagh had been put through to Sergeant Coady and finished briefing him as they got into their car.

'He was a thieving bastard all the same,' muttered Courtney in the back as he fastened his seat belt.

His two colleagues turned around with quizzical expressions.

'His toiletry bag,' he explained, 'he nicked one of those little hotel shampoos'.

Chapter 59

AJ had written many incident reports but she was finding this one particularly challenging. How did she explain how she found the murder site when she wasn't part of the investigation team? In fact, she was explicitly directed by the officer in charge to keep the fuck out of it. Assuming she did admit that she took an interest in the case because she was the one who actually opened the suitcase, how far back should she go? How much should she say? That she was devoting most of her on-duty and off-duty time to it? That she was following people around who she thought might be involved? That she had tried to bring her views on it to the attention of the lead investigator, but he wasn't interested? Should she include her other suspicions concerning this case?

Just this morning, after her making a significant breakthrough in the case less than twenty-four hours ago, Hennessy had dashed into the station and out again an hour later, without even acknowledging her existence.

She didn't know Pilger or Hannon, but she had had several conversations with Wang about the case. He was very complimentary of her contributions.

After several false starts, she decided to take a break and get some fresh air. Coady had come out to check that she was okay, but she just told him she was tired from all of the excitement the day before and from the gruesome scene she had uncovered.

Tim tried to take her mind off the murder case by telling her about the GNECB operation earlier.

'Seems some American celebrity counterfeiter was visiting our shores recently, a guy named Whitney,' he beamed.

'Did they arrest him?' asked AJ.

'No, he isn't wanted for anything. They were just checking if he was trying to bring funny money out of the country or if he had any tools of the trade in his luggage. Stopped him after he checked in and went through screening. Clean as a whistle and cool as a cucumber, according to one of the new officers in there. They're very respectful to the station, I have to say'.

'Long may it continue,' said AJ.

As they spoke, a large blue aircraft tail moved slowly behind them, under tow to one of the hangars. It was almost as if it was trying to sneak past them without alerting them to its two hundred tonnes presence.

AJ reflected a bit more on Tim's information.

'And he came in when did you say Tim, last week?'

'Last Thursday morning, I think, on one of the overnight US flights.

'So, four nights and he's a big enough player in the business for the Secret Service to keep an eye on him, and even let us know about his travels?'

'Appears so. Said he was just visiting but wouldn't say where. It's a pity they didn't pick him up or follow him on the way in, I suppose. Anyway, he's gone now,' said Tim.

'Thanks for the chat, Tim,' said AJ as she headed back into the station.

'Ready to finish that report now?' he queried.

'Absolutely, but I need to check something first.'

If at first, you don't succeed

did that victim need to bleed

what it took to seal her fate

the incident report will have to wait

Chapter 60

'The fuck does he want? I've heard that shit before,' fumed Hennessy when he was contacted by the officer securing his hospital room that Ger Cosgrave wanted to talk to him.

'I couldn't tell you, Detective Inspector, but he swears he's serious and that it's urgent. Will I tell him to fuck off?' asked the officer.

'Last I heard, he was suing me for maiming him, so yes, please do'.

Hennessy left the conference room with Lucas Hannon, and they both made their way over to the murder site. He was beginning to have grave doubts about Tobin being connected to the murder at all, in which case he was wasting his time dealing with either him or his useless sidekick Cosgrave.

'There's something acutely unedifying about revisiting a murder site', Hennessy said as they neared the crime scene tape.

'Although you know that your only interest is to catch the perpetrator, it still feels hugely uncomfortable at times to be standing there, staring continuously at where this young woman has been defiled. There's something almost ghoulish or voyeuristic about it, I believe. And doesn't it seem bizarre that less than fifty metres away, planes are landing and taking off as if all was normal?'

On the other side of the fence, a never-ending convoy of cars, vans, trucks, buses, and bicycles passed by, most of the occupants peering in at the hive of Garda activity.

'Jesus!' said Hannon taking in the area. 'How in the name of Christ did we ever find this?'

'We didn't, AJ did,' Hennessy answered honestly as his phone rang again.

He spoke to the caller for about thirty seconds and then hung up.

'I have to go, Lucas; I'll tune in with you later'.

Chapter 61

Sandra Whelan had proved an excellent teacher on the airport's CCTV system, AJ thought as she sat in front of the computer screen. Knowing where to find different parts of the airport on the footage and looking at specific dates and times proved very useful in her latest quest.

The starting point was straightforward. Tim had told her where and when the GNECB officers had picked the counterfeiter up for questioning, so she had quickly secured a distinct image of Rodney Whitney to work with.

That was the easy bit.

After spending over two hours carefully studying hundreds of passengers arriving off transatlantic flights and hundreds of people meeting them, her search had focused on the food court on the next floor. It was a laborious process looking at the same people from several different camera angles before ruling them in or out.

When AJ was happy she had what she needed, she emailed her results to a colleague in Headquarters.

It was an hour before her shift ended, so she decided to finish up her incident report before she clocked off. She also decided to be honest, not get anyone into trouble and at the same time be economical with the background and next steps.

She started typing.

Too much time spent worrying about others

too much energy on digging up the past

time to jettison all this band of brothers

sometimes partnerships just don't last

Chapter 62

'Is it true?'

Cosgrave's first question caught Hennessy off-guard; he hadn't even closed the door.

'Was Tobin on his way to kill me last night?'

'You tell me, Cosgrave, you're the fucking know-all around here?'

'Did you arrest him? What did he say?'

'I can't tell you any of those details, Cosgrave, you know fucking well I can't. Now, what do you want to see me about? You've got thirty seconds and I'm out of here.'

'There's only one cop outside my door. He can still get to me. You need to protect me, Hennessy, for fucks sake!' cried a frightened Cosgrave.

'Right, I'm gone, fuck off and die, Cosgrave.'

'Okay, okay. I'll tell you what you need to know about Tobin, but I want extra protection in here, and I want to go into the witness protection thing. Otherwise, I might as well kill meself.'

'I can't promise you anything, Cosgrave. It all depends on what you can give me. Last time I set up our legal people for your 'big confession', you fucked me over,' said Hennessy taking advantage of his upper hand.

'I can give you loads on Tobin; you'll have him hook, line and sinker'.

'Including his involvement with the murdered girl?' probed Hennessy.

'That's the thing. Tobin wasn't involved in that, as far as I know. But I'll give you enough where you can make sure for yourself, at least it rules him in or out. Plus, Tobin goes away for life either way?' said Cosgrave trying not to show his desperation.

Hennessy thought about it, letting Cosgrave sweat for a while.

'Right, you tell me what you know now, the condensed version. I'll get the legal people in to get it all down formally. I'll have you moved to the hospital wing in the Midlands, where you'll get protection. If you want me to make a case – and that's all I can do – to the Crime and Security Section in HQ to get you into the Witness Security Programme, you have to testify in court against Tobin. The WSP means you get a new identity in a different country, retraining, and a job'.

Now it was Cosgrave doing the thinking.

Hennessy reckoned Cosgrave was trying to figure out how he could give them the information they wanted without incriminating himself even more. They already had him on trafficking and pulling a gun on the Guards.

'What about the charges you're holding me on now?'

'I'll talk to the legal people. The refugees say you didn't harm them'.

I didn't get a chance; Cosgrave was thinking to himself.

'And pulling the gun?'

'You didn't fire it', said Hennessy.

I didn't get a chance.

Chapter 63

They weren't quite sure what they were looking for but Lorraine O'Keefe and Eamonn Kavanagh thought it might be worth following up.

When Lorraine rang the hotel, she couldn't get any information and realised that the receptionist thought it was a hoax call. Certainly, the request to speak to a manager got nowhere. They were busy with guests checking out.

It was only an hour from their office on Harcourt Street. After identifying themselves at Reception, Lorraine asked to speak to the Duty Manager. They were waiting only a few minutes before a well-dressed woman arrived and introduced herself as Agneta.

'We'd like to ask you a few questions about someone who may have stayed here last week?' asked Eamonn Kavanagh.

'Sure,' said Agneta pleasantly, 'but first, can I offer you tea or coffee, some scones?'

'No, thank you,' replied Lorraine, 'this won't take long. Can we ask you if the shampoos in your rooms have the hotel's name on them?'

Agneta's eyebrows raised in surprise. She obviously wasn't expecting this question from the Gardaí.

'Yes, we provide our guests with branded soaps, conditioners, shower gels and shampoos. 'The Gallops' is written in gold lettering with a smaller type underneath saying 'Kildare'. They're organic. Why, did someone complain?'

'Not at all,' said Lorraine quickly as she took a black and white photo out of her inside jacket pocket, 'do you recognise this man?'

'Yes, the American gentleman,' Agneta confirmed without hesitating.

'Can we ask you some questions about his stay, please? It might be beneficial for our investigation?' asked O'Keefe.

'What kind of questions?'

'Like, how many nights did he stay? Did he reserve the room or just turn up at the front desk? Was anyone with him? Did he pay for the room himself? Did he have a car? Did he ask your staff about any local attractions or for directions anywhere, or book a taxi? Do you have records of phone calls to or from his room? And your camera system, does it cover the restaurant and the car park at the front?'

'That's a lot of questions,' said Agneta, a little taken aback, 'and I'm not sure how much information I can release under GDPR rules. Can I call you back on it?'

'We'd prefer if we could gather any information we can while we're here, please, Agneta?' answered O'Keefe.

'Very well then,' agreed Agneta, 'I think maybe you should accept that tea and scones offer now?'

Chapter 64

Skip McEvoy was getting a bit worried about his mother.

This morning, she seemed weak when she came downstairs for breakfast, and her appetite had definitely been off these last few days.

Such thoughts didn't stop Skip from carrying out his usual checks when he pulled out of his front drive and drove around aimlessly for a few kilometres to ensure no one was following him.

Just after Heuston railway station, he decided he was satisfied, so he continued east on the Chapelizod bypass before turning left onto the R109. It wasn't raining, but the dark clouds foretold a heavy downpour soon. The thermometer on the car's dashboard read a wintery 6C.

McEvoy turned right onto Infirmary Road as he decided to bring his mother to the doctor this afternoon. He didn't believe in making appointments where his mother was concerned. If she wasn't seen immediately, someone else would need medical assistance.

He drove on autopilot thinking about her, making left and right turns automatically, pondering what might be wrong with her. She'd had her annual check-up in the Mater Private at the end of last year, and everything seemed fine, particularly for a lady of her vintage.

Maybe the stairs were getting to be a bit much lately; perhaps he should convert a room downstairs to a bedroom and move her down? He was considering this as he drove through two roundabouts and took a left turn onto Cappagh road.

He didn't want any of the neighbours to see her getting a little shaky, gossiping about her, besmirching her good name. He wouldn't have it. Not on his watch, he resolved as he took the second exit off the roundabout onto Finglaswood road and the third exit off the next roundabout bringing him onto Mellowes road.

Such was his concentration on his mother's health that the white VW van with the ladder on top following him onto Jamestown Road and again onto McKee Avenue went unnoticed.

The journey to Finglas had taken him thirty-three minutes. The row of eight empty garages was a sight he had become accustomed to over the last decade. Red-bricked with wooden doors, they had been constructed for the eight houses behind them, but when the houses were knocked down years ago to build apartments, the garage site was not needed by the developers. They were empty because they were all owned by the same person now, having been bought up one at a time over several years. Some of the owners were happy to sell, but two signed the contracts in the presence of their solicitors, from hospital beds.

All was quiet. Skip waited a few minutes to survey the area and see if anything had been disturbed since yesterday. Fully alert now.

Everything looked okay, so he got out of his car, locked it, and strolled over to the third garage down. It looked as rundown as the others, but the door had a double deadbolt lock and a metal skin on the inside.

He opened it quietly, stepped inside, and had begun engaging the heavy sliding bolt to close it when the bolt was ripped from his hands, and the door seemed to descend on him. Roars of 'ARMED GARDAÍ, DOWN!' assaulted his ears. He fell away from the door, a hard boot catching him in the back and helping him on his way. As soon as he hit the ground, a knee pinned him there. Skip McEvoy's arms were pulled forcefully behind his back and handcuffed, making his head turn sideways, facing the metal cage in the far corner.

Chapter 65

He preferred meeting Brophy when her personal assistant, McAllister, wasn't there taking notes. Nothing personal against McAllister, but the formality of it made Hennessy feel uncomfortable. There were just the two of them in Brophy's office. As promised, she returned his firearm.

'So, you have two active crime scenes since we spoke last and two new arrests?'

'That's correct, ma'am, the airport and a garage in Finglas. And we've arrested Alphie Tobin, and a guy named Skip McEvoy. Ger Cosgrave agreed to cooperate with us after Tobin was arrested, and he gave us the heads-up on McEvoy'.

'And you rescued two more refugees?'

'Yes, McEvoy had two men locked up in a cage. They're from Afghanistan and speak decent English, I'm told.'

'Take me through where we are then'.

'According to Cosgrave, and he's probably lying about his own role, Tobin has been trafficking people through an intermediary in Germany and selling them on to different gangs around the country'.

'That's where Tobin was coming from the day the body was found?'

'From Berlin, but McEvoy says Tobin came back early because a group of seven were diverted into Belfast when the traffickers ran into problems getting them into England. So, he had to fly back on Sunday instead of Wednesday to sort it out. We're checking flight records and his phone to verify that'.

'And it just so happens that a girl is found butchered as he was coming through? Maybe he was bringing back one of the refugees on the flight, and she acted up, so he did away with her at the airport?'

'There's no record of her being on any of the flights that day, and there's no video footage of her getting off any of them, ma'am. Cosgrave says Tobin didn't kill the girl but that she may have been murdered to set him up, ma'am?'

'But Tobin came back unexpectedly?' she queried.

'Which means they were following Tobin's movements very closely. Still, it does make sense ma'am, that Tobin wouldn't deliberately travel through an airport at the same time as a girl that he killed turns up. Plus, if he was set up, they would have made sure there was evidence connecting him to the victim?'

'Maybe Tobin had her killed and dumped on Sunday because he was supposed to be out of the country and couldn't stop the plan in time when he had to fly back early?' suggested Brophy, not really believing it herself.

'Or maybe the murder and Tobin's trafficking operation are unconnected, ma'am?' said Hennessy, wanting to make the point before Brophy did even though he had been the one pushing Tobin as the prime suspect from day one.

'Too big a coincidence surely, as you've been arguing, Detective?' she replied.

'Not so much maybe if Tobin did travel back early and at short notice, and we're trying to establish that now. Suppose Tobin had flown in three days after the body was discovered ma'am, would we ever have linked him to it without any evidence?'

Hennessy knew he was backtracking on many of the theories he had come up with to point at Tobin, but none of them had panned out, so he figured it was better to get it out there.

'Which brings us back to who did kill her, and of course, who is she?' said Brophy even though her tone suggested she was wondering why he'd been wasting the investigation's fucking time for the last ten fucking days?

'Well, there may be a lead on the second part of that question, ma'am. According to Cosgrave, Skip McEvoy is a dealer'.

'In girls?' asked Brophy.

'In anything, ma'am. Drugs, girls, boys, cars, bikes, anything people want. He has a long record but mainly for assaults and possession of stolen equipment. It seems that when one of the seven refugees went missing, Tobin sent Cosgrave to get one from Skip McEvoy'.

'Get one, as in, get a girl to replace the one that was arrested for nearly killing a police officer? Get a girl just like you'd go out to get a bag of chips?'

'Yes, ma'am. Tobin's deal was to sell on a group of seven to some gang in Munster but McEvoy wanted too much money and wanted it all upfront, without showing them what they were buying'.

'Christ, what kind of a society are we living in? What kind of fucking animals do we inhabit this country with?' asked Brophy.

Hennessy didn't reply. He was a bit surprised that Brophy was so shocked; she had worked in Serious Crimes for a few years.

'Cosgrave reckons if someone in Dublin wanted to get an untraceable person, for whatever purpose, McEvoy was the man to go to. I've sent Hannon to interview the Afghans as he dealt with the other refugees, and Calvin Walsh redeployed two technicians from the airport site to the garage. The murdered girl may have been held in that cage at some point. Maybe a long shot I know, but McEvoy doesn't seem the type to clean up after himself every time he moves someone on'.

Brophy was still looking down at her desk when Hennessy's phone got a text message.

'That's from Jenny Pilger, ma'am. Tobin did change his flight on Sunday morning to fly back that day instead of Wednesday'.

Chapter 66

Leah Regan was on the public counter when AJ arrived in, the conference room in use again.

'Would you say they're armed, AJ?'

'Who?'

'Those English coppers in there, very serious-looking dudes, deadly dressers'.

'Dunno, depends on what was agreed with our people. There's usually a few of them allowed to carry weapons for VIP visits, but I thought that was only on the day'.

Leah was about to say something else but was interrupted by an elderly man coming in to report a stolen passport. AJ heard a part of the conversation and was glad it happened on the home leg rather than on the outward journey. She always felt it was easier to deal with when you were home instead of having your trip ruined before it started.

Flicking through her emails, AJ found a response to a request she had made the previous day. She quickly picked up the phone.

'Liam, AJ, you found him?'

AJ had worked with Liam Cheevers in Tralee for a few months when they were assigned to a task force set up to tackle two feuding gangs in the area, one of which had terrorist links. Liam had acted as a tourist guide for some of the officers involved as he was born in Annascaul on the Dingle Peninsula. He had followed his father and grandfather in joining the force and was now working in the National Crime and Security Intelligence Service.

'I'm fine, thanks AJ, good of you to ask,' he replied jokingly.

'Sorry Liam, I hope everything is going well in that big job in those lovely offices overlooking Phoenix Park. Now, who is he?'

'A Romanian guy named Florin Ardelean, involved in various scams: ATM fraud, money laundering, dealing in stolen goods, that sort of thing. He's served a few short sentences. Claims to run a legit import/export business.

We've a few different addresses for him; I'll email them and some of the people we think he hangs out with'.

'Appreciate that, thanks Liam'.

'AJ?' he asked before she could hang up.

'Yes?'

'Are you back in the investigations business; I thought you were taking a bit of a breather at the airport?' he queried.

'Just doing my bit Liam, cheers,' she answered and quickly hung up, already looking up another number on her laptop for a name Tim Coady had given her.

'Hello, my name is Anna Jenkinson from the Dublin airport station. You had a few people here yesterday, and I'm trying to follow up with one of them: Eamonn Kavanagh?'

The person answering said he wasn't there but gave AJ his mobile number.

'Hello, Eamonn Kavanagh? My name is Anna Jenkinson from the station at Dublin airport. You were talking to my colleague, Sergeant Coady, yesterday. I just wanted to follow up on something, if you don't mind?'

Eamonn was sitting beside Lorraine on their way back from The Gallops Hotel.

'Sure, fire away'.

'That guy you stopped yesterday, Whitney, do you know what he was doing here?'

'Well, he said he was a tourist travelling around the place but we've just been to the one hotel that he spent the four nights in, and he sure didn't travel very far. Back for dinner every night, even lunch on one day, that sort of thing. Said he left a broken wheelie bag in his room, and that wasn't true either'.

'Where is that?' AJ asked as she opened the email that just came in from Cheevers.

'To quote one of the tourist leaflets at Reception, 'in the hills and hollows of the 5,000 acres Curragh of Kildare',' he rolled off lyrically.

Bingo, thought AJ as she read the email.

Faces in a crowd

mothers looking proud

in amongst the mayhem

Anna spots a rare gem

Chapter 67

It didn't matter how many times he visited; the same discomfort engulfed him. Calvin Walshe was still beavering away, and there were several other white-suited individuals diligently poking and peering at various pieces of equipment. The skies were darkening as nightfall was setting in.

Walshe noticed him and came over, removing his face mask as he walked.

'Plenty of work going on Cal, anything new?' asked Hennessy.

Walshe started to answer but the thunderous shriek of an aircraft landing forced him to lower his ear muffs. When it abated, he held out the headgear to Hennessy.

'First time I had to order these for my staff!'

'Two of whom you had to send to Finglas earlier; thanks for that, I know you're stretched,' said Hennessy.

'We all are, Gar; your guy had to head off earlier as well'.

'More refugees to interview. You're gathering a lot of material here, Calvin,' said Hennessy scanning the area, 'I hope we get a hit'.

'Hard to say. We have loads of prints and DNA, sure, but this equipment spends its long life being handled by hundreds of people, and the DNA may all be from one person, the victim'.

'Plus, assuming the cart she was murdered in has been here since Sunday, the heavy rain and freezing nights since then probably didn't help?'

'That cart was surprisingly well sealed up actually, probably to deter anyone from peeking in; pretty much watertight, so there was hardly any degradation in the samples that we've processed so far'.

'So the two maintenance tools?' asked Hennessy.

'No degradation but no prints and only the girl's DNA; they were wearing gloves'.

'Which we haven't found, despite putting more people on it and expanding the search area to airport-wide'.

'Rubbish trucks are coming and going all the time, Gar, so I'd be surprised if anything turned up. Plus, of course, there's an incinerator here'.

'Yeah, I know,' said an increasingly despondent Hennessy as another aircraft landed on the main runway, the sharp braking action making it veer ever so slightly to the left, as though it was sneaking a peek at the offending baggage trolley.

Another patrol car parked close to the yellow tape, and Pilger and Wang got out.

'We heard you were here, boss, so said we'd head over to give you an update,' said Pilger as they approached, 'which won't take long to be honest'.

'So, nothing?' asked Hennessy.

'Nothing so far on the two cleaning staff. No criminal records and no family ties with any. Good attendance levels, no disciplinary issues. They both have negative bank balances, but nothing dramatic. Their credit ratings are not Bill Gates' standard but not disastrous. If somebody was paying them to misbehave in some way last Sunday, either it was in cash, or it hasn't been lodged to their account yet. I'm still digging boss, but I'm getting less hopeful,' said Pilger.

'No big breakthroughs on my side either,' said Wang getting in quickly with the bad news before Hennessy could respond to Pilger. 'Sure, there are lots of baggage cart convoys heading all over the place, but I can't find any visiting this site, not with the brutal CCTV coverage here. And there are lots of images of people walking around, particularly on the freezing nights when the snow and ice crews are active, but no one that I can identify as coming here'.

'I've loads of people throwing bags and stuff into bins and into the incinerator, but that's standard practice at an airport; that's what they're paid to do. I'm narrowing those pictures down to the window we're interested in the night of the murder, but then again, that might be too obvious. They might have deliberately hidden a plastic bag full of blood-soaked clothes somewhere and then dumped it the next day or two days later. You don't even have to hide it around here; you could leave it in plain sight; there is any amount of them. Sandra Whelan told me that the average flight has six full bags of rubbish taken off it, and nearly a quarter of a million flights came in and out last year'.

'Thanks, Wang, that's really fucking cheered me up!'

'That info on Tobin changing flights any good boss?' asked Pilger, knowing the answer.

'Good for him, alright, Jenny,' replied Hennessy with sarcasm.

As the three detectives stood shuffling their feet and pulling their coats tighter against the cold, a white and green wide-body jet trudged slowly past them, taxiing to the end of the runway to turn around and take-off.

'I'm gonna check in with Hannon,' shouted Hennessy looking at the aircraft, 'before that fucker bursts my eardrums'.

He took the designated perimeter roadway directly to the boundary gate opened and staffed by the Airport Police specifically to facilitate the Garda operation at the luggage cart site.

Turning right on to Collinstown Lane brought him back up past the murder site on the land side towards the M50 motorway that acted as a ring road around the city.

He was about to press Lucas Hannon's number on speed dial when he decided that he could no longer avoid having the conversation that would answer the question. The question that Brophy hadn't asked him, that Hannon, Pilger and Wang were aching to ask him: how the fuck did Jenkinson find the luggage cart?

The revs and acceleration told him it must be Matusz, but the poor lighting made it hard to confirm. He had just separated from AJ to check the bins and raced across in time to see her lying on the ground, taking aim at the car.

He shouted at her not to fire. He was afraid the child was in the car, but two shots rang out as the driver braked to take a sharp left and then a right to exit the car park. The car skidded and hit another vehicle on the corner about fifty metres away.

AJ was up and running when Hennessy was still cursing her for opening fire. She got to the car first. The driver's door was wide open, but there was no sign of him.

She slowly opened the boot and had just caught a glimpse of a yellow dress when she was grabbed from behind and a knife pressed against her throat. Matusz spun her around as Hennessy reached the scene.

'The girl is mine,' screamed Matusz.

Hennessy was pointing his revolver at him in a two-handed firing position.

'Put the knife down and let her go,' said Hennessy in a low voice, trying to be as calm as he could.

The lighting was better around the exit, and he could clearly see that it was Matusz and that he looked manic.

'No one takes the girl from me,' he shouted, strengthening his hold of AJ.

'Shoot him, Garry, shoot the fucker!' she roared.

Sweat was running down Hennessy's back. He was trying to hold the gun steady, but his grip was shaking.

'Shoot!' yelled AJ again.

She was looking into Hennessy's eyes, and the fear in them told her he wasn't going to take the shot.

Hennessy could see AJ's expression change; she knew.

Summoning all her energy, she freed her right arm and elbowed Matusz in the ribs. He loosened his hold and she spun around, grabbed the arm holding the knife and twisted it violently around his back, tripping him with her right leg and pinning him down with her knee.

Chapter 68

The side of the building had no lighting whatsoever, and every step felt like it was going to land on a twig or broken glass. AJ was checking for cameras and motion-activated security lights. The other units in the industrial park looked like they were closed up for the night.

Adrenalin is double-edged, she thought; it makes you sharper, but it also makes you shake.

The back of the building had no cameras, lights or doors either. That left one side and the front. She could see an entry at the third side of the building near the front with a camera positioned above, pointing directly down. Her phone vibrated in her pocket, but she ignored it. Instead, she moved away from the building along a low wall from where she could survey the side door and the sliding vehicle entrance at the front. It had two spotlights and a camera overhead.

There was a light on inside, but she couldn't hear any movements or voices. She shivered. It was cold, and her uniform wasn't providing much insulation. She needed to get closer and was working her way over to the side door when headlights appeared on the entrance road. She got back down behind the wall. Again, her phone vibrated to indicate a call.

When the white car drove up to the sliding roller door, two powerful spotlights lit up the forecourt. A man came out of the side door, wheeling a bag. It was hard to see him clearly. The man who got out of the car, however, she did recognise. Either no words were exchanged between the two men, or they were spoken quietly.

This looked like it would be a short transaction between the two men, so she decided to act. She touched the handcuffs on the left-hand side of her uniform belt and the extendable baton on the right.

She had reached the edge of the lit-up area before they saw her.

'Gardaí! On the ground, you're under arrest!' she shouted as confidently as she could.

The two men were startled and peered through the shadows to spot other Gardaí. Their alarmed expressions turned a little more smug when they realised there was only AJ.

'Jenkinson? What the fuck are you doing?' yelled Tony Gibbons.

'Arresting two murderers Gibbons, down on the ground'.

'Doesn't look like you're armed, Jenkinson? In fact, from what I hear, you're lucky to be still wearing the uniform. Fucked up, didn't you, shooting at a car with a child in it?' said Gibbons growing in confidence.

She could see that Florin Ardelean was getting jumpy, constantly twisting around, and trying to figure out his best move.

'There's no point in even thinking about it,' she said quickly. 'Step away from the bag and get down on the ground, now!'

The two men still weighed up their options.

'We didn't murder anyone; what are you talking about?' asked Ardelean.

'Where do I start, the armed robbery or the murder?' AJ replied, deciding that she needed to play for time.

'Baggage belt number 7, the only one that can be accessed at a particular point without getting picked up on CCTV, so that someone can lift a suitcase onto it unseen. The know-how and contacts to stop maintenance going ahead on that belt. Meeting in The Ark the next morning to suss out the rumours circulating. Then there's the plastic sheeting that you tried to wrap around the girl; it was in the suitcase and luggage cart. That's from the rolls in the sorting hall for putting on broken baggage. Is that all the poor girl was to you fuckers, a broken bag?'

'Wait, wait,' interrupted Gibbons, 'that's not on us'.

'The fuck it isn't! The fake currency in the bag you're wheeling; was that what it was all about? Butchering a girl so that you can make some funny money, fucking pathetic bastards!'

She was trying her luck now but they looked more panicked, so she had to keep talking.

'Didn't need a genius to work it out. The guy who can access all areas at the airport, including the cargo terminal, so that boxes can be left in particular spots. The air waybill had the TransEuro stamp for handler. The airport of origin code was OTP; isn't that Bucharest in Romania Ardelean? A master forger arriving from the States a few days later; is that his bag? So I'm guessing it was a specialised forgery printer in those two crates, and it's still in the warehouse behind you? The origin and weight would be about right, and you're smuggling the forged currency out of the country tonight by the same route?'

They were both looking like making a move, so AJ kept talking, still unsure if her guesses were correct.

'What are you planning to use it for in Romania, Ardelean? Is it easier to launder money there? Do you swap it for drugs or guns? You do dabble in a lot of criminal activities, after all? In fact, why make the counterfeit money here at all; why not leave the machine in Romania and send Whitney there? Is he wanted there? Denied a visa?'

'Why didn't you arrest him if you thought he was here to forge currency?' asked a nervous Ardelean, edging a little bit closer to her.

'Simple. The guards who interviewed him didn't know about this operation but don't worry, our colleagues in the Secret Service will be calling'.

She needed to start moving forward or backwards; she couldn't keep the lid on their panic much longer.

Ardelean took the decision out of her hands, pulling a knife from his waistband and approaching her.

'Enough, you fucking bitch!'

AJ backed away slowly. Gibbons was waiting anxiously to see the outcome.

When the Romanian was seconds from reaching striking distance, another scream.

'Armed Gardaí, down on the ground, drop the fucking knife!'

Lorraine O'Keefe emerged slowly from the darkness on the left with her gun pointed at Ardelean.

On the right, Eamonn Kavanagh made sure Gibbons dispelled any notions of fleeing.

A cruel twist of fate

maybe it's too late

have to make up time

need to solve the crime

Earlier, Eamonn Kavanagh was still in the office when AJ called.

'AJ again. Wanna' help me check out a place near the hotel where Whitney might have been working?'

'Hold on'. She heard Kavanagh whispering excitedly to Lorraine O'Keefe.

'Fuck yes!'

'Great. I'll text you the address. Don't park within sight of the building and don't approach from the front'.

'Not our first rodeo AJ'.

She was about to hang up when Eamonn spoke again.

'AJ, do you have a search warrant?'

'Fuck no!'

Chapter 69

She was checking her phone as she rushed back to the car. Kavanagh and O'Keefe had arrested the two criminals and taken them back to Dublin to be processed. They confirmed that the wheelie bag contained bundles of forged $100 bills and a crude-looking printer in the warehouse. Local Gardaí were on the scene, and a technical team en-route.

The two missed calls were from Hennessy, then he had sent a text.

'We need to talk'.

Her response was equally succinct.

'Airport. Another arrest to make'.

The temptation to ring him as she drove back was resisted by her need to complete the picture. It was too soon to summarise things, too many unknowns.

Garda Avril Travers was the only officer on duty when AJ got back. The light was on in the conference room, but the blinds were drawn, so it was hard to see who the occupants were.

As soon as she sat down, Travers asked her if she minded holding the fort while she conducted a patrol.

'Sure, Avril, go ahead'.

She put her two hands out on the desk. She was still pumped up from Kildare, but she needed to think. Think AJ, think, think, she said to herself.

What's my next move, and who do I go for first, she asked herself.

After a few minutes, she slapped her right hand on the desk.

'Fuck it, whoever's nearer!' she muttered.

She looked up numbers on her phone and then made three calls: the first to the passenger terminal, then the car park, and finally the Airport Police.

Having waited another five minutes, she got up and walked the short distance to the staff car park in front of the old central terminal building.

All the streetlights were working, but the heavy mist swirling around made for poor visibility. In addition, the chill in the evening air seemed to heighten the noxious scent of aviation fumes.

AJ kept to the shadows near a particular car. A few minutes later, a woman hurried over from the passenger terminal and started checking the car, carefully examining the windscreen and windows.

'The car is fine, Eileen,' said AJ stepping into view.

Eileen Gleeson looked petrified.

'They told me someone broke into it. Who are you? What do you want?' asked Eileen, recognising AJ from around the airport, her words rapid and her voice high-pitched.

'I know,' said AJ.

'Know what? What are you talking about? What did you bring me out here for?'

'Belt number 7. The smell when there was no smell. I watched the footage. You pretended to look around for a bit but you were always heading for one place: belt 7,' AJ explained.

The alarm on Gleeson's face wasn't dimmed by the mist.

'Listen to me, Eileen,' AJ went on, 'you don't have to take all the blame. I know you were told what to do. If you cooperate- '

'Shut fucking up, Jenkinson! Eileen, come over here!' growled a voice from AJ's right.

'So, you turned up?' asked AJ calmly, looking at him, and the firearm in his right hand pointed at her, having already thought through this scenario as best she could.

'I told you to shut up! Eileen, get in the car, we're going'.

Eileen looked at AJ and then looked at the man on her left. Uncertainty replaced alarm in her expression.

'Your old contacts in the Bureau was it, who told you about the arrests in the Curragh?'

AJ had asked Lorraine and Eamonn to keep the arrests off the airwaves for a few hours if they could but she knew how quickly these things got around the force. She also knew the man on her right had worked in money laundering in the same Bureau as the counterfeiting unit.

'Eileen, he didn't come here to rescue you. He came here to make sure you didn't talk to us,' said AJ in a sympathetic tone.

'Jenkinson, one more fucking word and I'll put a fucking bullet between your eyes!' he barked.

She needed to take advantage of his anger. That's what they had taught her in Templemore: anger blurs focus.

'You murdered an innocent young girl for a few quid, you prick!'

'It wasn't like that,' he blurted, 'that wasn't the plan'.

'What was the plan, to educate her, put her through college, find her a partner?' asked AJ in disgust. Nevertheless, she could see she was making progress; she needed to keep pushing.

'The message said a big package was coming through, so we thought it was drugs, like before. We needed to divert attention away from the cargo terminal and get the Customs sniffer dog up to the passenger terminal'.

He was talking freely now, as if almost pleased to get it off his chest.

'We wanted a man, a big guy, so that he could resist arrest when he was caught, create a kerfuffle like. But McEvoy said it'd have to be a girl. Charged a fortune'.

AJ didn't know who McEvoy was but she didn't want to interrupt the flow, so she continued to stare at the man.

'Gibbo smuggled her airside easily; he can come and go in the company vans all day without being checked. She spoke some English but not a lot. When we told her all she had to do was say the bag was hers, we promised her that it would be fine. She'd be arrested for drug possession but it was only a tiny amount in the bag, and she could claim political asylum as soon as they took her to the station. We said we were doing her a favour. That otherwise, McEvoy would sell her to some gang to work in a brothel. This was her chance'.

He was breathing heavily now, and AJ was worried he might clam up.

'So you battered her and sliced her up with aircraft tools when she refused?' she asked, to coax him on. Just another little bit, she thought.

'She started sobbing and saying 'no drugs, no drugs'. She was getting louder and going to attract attention. That fucking bitch could have blown it all!'

He rubbed his forehead with his left arm; he wasn't pointing the gun straight anymore.

'We had to shut her up, so we told her it was okay, we wouldn't force her. We said we'd smuggle her off the airport again in a baggage cart, and then we'd drive her to a Garda station. She could claim political asylum'.

'But that was never going to happen,' said AJ, still trying to eke out more information.

'We couldn't risk her telling anyone. She had seen Gibbo and me. So when she climbed into the cart and sat down....'

He was drifting now; how much further can I go? AJ asked herself.

'But why not leave her in the dolly? Why stuff the poor thing into a suitcase and put her on the baggage conveyor?' One last piece, please, she thought.

'Because we still needed to cause trouble in the passenger terminal. But the plan was falling apart. There was blood everywhere, and the bag was a bastard to close. We needed to dump our clothes, and I needed to get offsite. I was dressed up as a handler, the full uniform, and a big hood. The message to ring cleaning wasn't changed; it still said smell. We got all the focus on the passenger terminal all right but it was too much, too many guards around, so the normal crew the boss used to collect cargo got scared; it was too risky. They had to change the plan and rob the boxes the next day. And after all that, it wasn't drugs he was bringing in this time; it was a fucking printer!'

AJ saw that Eileen was now bent over weeping and that he was distracted, so she pretended to move towards Eileen with her arms out to comfort her and planned to smash him across the head with her right arm. She was almost there when a roar from her left changed the plan.

'Put the gun down, Hannon!' yelled Hennessy.

Lucas Hannon reacted at speed, grabbing AJ around the neck and putting his gun to her right temple.

'Don't think so, boss. Eileen, get in the fucking car and start it, now!'

Eileen stared at her lover, fear and loathing spreading across her face.

'I won't hesitate, Hannon, you're a fucking disgrace! You told Tobin about the raid in Balbriggan,' shouted Hennessy, trying to control the shake in his hands.

'Cosgrave, not Tobin. I thought Tobin was there. It suited us to have you going gung-ho after Tobin. It meant you weren't chasing us'.

'You've shamed the job; you're nothing but a common killer. Drop your weapon,' said Hennessy.

'Started off small. Divorce debt and all. Before you know it...'

AJ noticed that Eileen was backing away. Hannon must have spotted her because his grip tightened. He was getting ready to start shooting.

She looked at Hennessy. His eyes were focused.

'Shoot him, Garry, shoot the fucker!' she screamed.

Hennessy fired, and milliseconds later, Hannon responded.

AJ saw Hennessy fall back against a car and felt Hannon shudder slightly. She freed her right arm and lashed out, striking him across the neck. He stumbled backwards, losing his hold on her.

Eileen turned and ran back towards the passenger terminal.

AJ raced across the car park to the station. He was right behind her. She flung open the door, ran behind the counter and tapped in the code for the gun safe.

The handle wouldn't turn.

Fuck, fuck, fuck, she thought as she realised the code had changed. It was changed every week for security reasons. She bent down behind the counter and searched for the folder with the code updates.

The front door was kicked in, and a gunshot hit the wall behind her. AJ fell forwards and scurried on all fours down the corridor into the conference room.

Chairs were lying on the ground, and people were huddled under the dark brown hardwood table. It was about twelve feet long and had wooden panel supports underneath.

AJ bundled in under the table, her pulse racing.

Hannon walked past the counter, noted the closed gun safe, and continued to the conference room. His stride was confident, determined. He pushed the door and swept the room with his gun.

The man crouched beside AJ had his legs scrunched up against a panel. AJ noticed him slowly moving back the right flap on his jacket. She didn't recognise his face.

Hannon started to walk towards the table.

Suddenly, AJ sprang out sideways and fired two shots at his legs as she hit the ground.

Hannon gasped with pain and crashed awkwardly to the floor, most of his gun arm pinned under his body.

As he struggled to free it, AJ darted over and stood on his wrist, then pistol-whipped him across his left temple.

A girl without a friend

an act against the trend

a wound too deep to mend

a life too young to end.

The good will learn to cope

the brave will cut the rope

the wise will see the scope

the humble will live in hope

Chapter 70

Half of the station was still a crime scene when AJ arrived on Wednesday afternoon. Nevertheless, she was eager to start working on her report while the events were still fresh in her mind.

Calvin Walshe saw her and beckoned her in, lifting the crime scene tape to access her desk. He had a mask on, but she could see from his eyes that he was smiling at her.

There was one other officer, Malachy Carter, in the station, and he had a cheerful wave for her.

She hadn't heard yet if she had caused a diplomatic incident by grabbing a Royal Protection detective's Glock 17 and discharging it. Nice suit.

The two shots both hit Hannon in the right tibia and shattered it. Multiple operations would be required to save the leg below the knee but he would still have a noticeable limp for the rest of his days.

Hennessy was doing better. The bullet missed major organs, but he lost a lot of blood. He hoped to be released from the hospital in a few days to recuperate at home. AJ had texted him last night: *thanks for taking the shot.*

An hour ago, he replied: *I missed.*

Sandra Whelan had texted her as well with a hearty note of congratulations. AJ felt guilty now for checking Sandra's laptop and mobile, but she had to be sure.

She unlocked the top drawer under her desk and took out an envelope. The address read: 'Detective Sergeant Anna Jenkinson, Garda Station, Dublin Airport'. The photograph inside showed a smiling mother and daughter behind a birthday cake. Turning over the photo, she read the simple note that she had read many times:

'Thank you AJ. Lots of love, Maja'.

As she put the envelope back and locked the drawer, her phone rang.

'AJ, Dougie, I think the diesel thief is back'.

If you enjoyed this book, could you please write a short review on Amazon?

COMING SOON, Book 2: *These roads he walked*

Printed in Poland
by Amazon Fulfillment
Poland Sp. z o.o., Wrocław

76651053R00221